MAVIS THOMAS

ENCHANTED VOYAGE

Complete and Unabridged

LINFORD
Leicester

First published in Great Britain in 2010

First Linford Edition
published 2010

British Library CIP Data

Thomas, Mavis.
    Enchanted voyage. - -
    (Linford romance library)
    1. Cruise ships- -Fiction. 2. Love stories.
    3. Large type books.
    I. Title II. Series
    823.9′14–dc22

    ISBN 978–1–44480–185–9

Published by
F. A. Thorpe (Publishing)
Anstey, Leicestershire

Set by Words & Graphics Ltd.
Anstey, Leicestershire
Printed and bound in Great Britain by
T. J. International Ltd., Padstow, Cornwall

This book is printed on acid-free paper

ENCHANTED VOYAGE

Lauren was a reluctant member of the family holiday group on a sea cruise, taking in Italy, Greece and Turkey. All her thoughts were of him: she agonised over Grant's accident, his operation, and his forthcoming marriage — to Elaine . . . However, whilst on the *Bella Italia*, Lauren became deeply involved with a charismatic member of the entertainment team . . . and a fellow passenger — a teacher and his two difficult children . . .

1

'Lauren, I know it's 5 a.m. and you'd rather have stayed in bed — but can't you just try to wipe that frown off your face?' My cousin Tina Milroy took a hand from her steering wheel to poke me in the ribs. 'Come on! We're almost at the Airport, isn't that just a teeny bit exciting?'

'Sorry,' I apologised. 'I know I'm being a wet blanket. And it's so good of you to drive me here, I'm really grateful.'

'I should hope so. Especially as I'm green with envy. Tell you what, let's swap places — I'll board your plane to the sunshine, you take over my office desk. Good idea, yes?'

'No!' I confessed, and we both laughed.

A few years my senior, she had always been more like a sister than a cousin, and at present we were sharing a London flat. Along the years, our paths had diverged quite a lot. Tina had waded through law exams and was now settled in a good career. My own goals had been very different — and mildly achieved, as evidenced by a small pile of concert programmes announcing 'Piano Recital by Lauren Roache,' 'Lauren Roache Plays Favourite Melodies' and so on. The most recent handful were titled 'A Musical Experience with Lauren Roache and Grant Standing'. Then, they came to an abrupt end.

Grant had been a fellow student at the Music College. At that time we were always together, and it had seemed to me love and music were bound up in one wondrous whole. But Grant moved away, we drifted apart. It was only last year that we met up again.

Only, this time it was different. This time, Grant was engaged to be married.

I couldn't quite say whose idea it was that the two of us try out a musical 'double act'. Certainly, I never expected we would strike gold! Grant had relegated his music to a sideline hobby, and was working in his father's stationery company — dull but steady, he said, necessary for a mortgage and a family.

But out of the blue, the instant success of our '*Musical Experience*' brought offers of theatre dates, TV dates, exciting tours. Grant's soulful violin, as well as his personal charm and classic good looks, had much to do with that. And briefly, so very briefly, life was a dream again.

The first warning shadow was his fiancee Elaine, wildly jealous of my stealing him away and diverting him from their planned future. It was a fateful threesome that couldn't endure. But surely, if my professional partnership with Grant brought money to spare for her to choose and furnish their home, she could have been a little more supportive? Surely she could have gloried in his success, maybe come on tour with us to share the hard work and excitement instead of sulking and fretting back in London?

She could have done that. But time sped by so rapidly, and none of us knew that just around the corner lay a cruel and unforgiving heartbreak . . .

'Gatwick, here we come!' Tina was saying cheerfully. 'Just run it past me again, Lauren, how many are going on this fabulous trip?'

I counted on my fingers. 'Aunt Dee, of course, it's all her doing. And she couldn't leave her sister home alone, so Aunt Ruby's coming too — though how she'll manage on a cruise ship I can't imagine, the poor dear gets seasick sitting by the garden pond. And that neighbour of theirs who's been helping out when they weren't too well — Hayden Somebody. Plus his child Jamie, who has asthma, I believe. Oh, and Jamie's older sister Alicia, who's your typical problem teenager. That was all at the last count.'

'Sounds like a barrel of laughs,' Tina approved. 'It'll shake you up, my dear.'

4

That prophecy was just what Aunt Delia had in her shrewd and caring mind when she first rang to announce I must join her party. 'All booked, Lauren, I got a good last minute deal on the cabins — my birthday present to you! No quibbles, I *need* you along to help with Ruby. So just go shopping for something gorgeous to wear in the sunshine, love, it'll do you a world of good after . . . '

She had no need to specify that 'after'. After the horror that befell Grant, that had brought me inescapable remorse.

'It's really important you come, because I've another job for you,' my wily Aunt had insisted. 'Hayden is having problems with his daughter — she's only about twelve though she looks sixteen-plus. I want you to sort the young madam out! She'd look on me as an interfering old biddy, but you might get through to her. Her Dad has been very good to Ruby and me, it would be something in return — you see?'

I saw, but it sounded an unlikely task for someone with zero experience of difficult children, whose life was already dominated by personal troubles. I made just one last protest: 'Aunt Dee, it's sweet of you, but — how can I go swanning off like this when — when Grant . . .'

'Grant would want you to go. He'd tell me to drag you on to the boat by your ears if I have to! So no more objections. All done and dusted!'

Done and dusted, settled and sorted. A refusal would have been too hurtfully churlish. So here I was now, surveying the Sussex landscape in the drowsy early morning — *very* early morning — en route for a flight to Italy.

The pleasant summer greenery was already giving way to the expanse of the Airport. No drowsiness here, indeed, with assorted planes flaunting their coloured tails on the tarmac, people busy and bustling. I drew one last resigned breath as Tina began bundling my luggage out of the car.

'There you go, you lucky girl! Grab that trolley that someone's dumped — I'll park and see you all inside, right?'

'Right,' I agreed. 'You're an angel, did you know that?'

She flashed me her bright, brisk smile.

Plenty of other folk had left their beds to be here queuing and fumbling for tickets, toting baggage, rounding up over-excited children. But I had no need to search the busy concourse for familiar faces. A voice hailed me at once, causing several heads to turn.

'Yoo-hoo, dear! Coo-ee! — '

Delia Roache, small and slight and energetic, kind of face and fluffy-grey of hair, was my father's sister and very dear to me. Since I lost my mother when I was just a toddler, she had tried with heart and soul to fill that huge emptiness; and after my father tragically died in an accident a couple of years on, she devoted her whole life to me. I never lacked for warm, supporting

7

arms, a listening ear. It was she who encouraged my musical education, she who turned up at every concert venue to clap her hands sore for encores. For her, I would do anything in the world.

'You're looking better, Laurie.' She peered with doubtful approval into my face. 'But still peaky, we must put that right. Come on, let's check your luggage in — and then we must rescue Hayden, he's in that café place in charge of the gang. No small task!' She winked at me one of her private wicked winks. 'Your Aunt Ruby isn't in holiday mood.'

'Oh dear. Are you sure it's a good idea to — '

'To drag her along? There's a special reason — a big secret, even from you! It mayn't work out, but I'm hoping. Mercy on us, what did you pack in this bag?'

'A lot,' I confessed. 'I couldn't get my head round what was best to bring.'

She patted my arm. 'Never mind, you'll be needing all sorts. We'll all have fun seeing the sights, and swimming and sunning, and playing deck quoits or whatever they do on these boats — '

'Even Aunt Ruby?' I suggested, and we shared a giggle.

I was soon being steered across the busy concourse to a refreshment area, to nod a greeting to the gloomy-faced elderly lady who sat clutching a capacious black handbag. Aunt Ruby Pym was a formidable figure, as bulky as Aunt Dee was petite, as severe of aspect as her sister was bright and cheery. They had lived together since Aunt Ruby's husband Tom died some-time back; with myself grown up and accounted for, Aunt Dee — being her ever-caring self — was ready for new responsibilities. I knew that medications and diets were the order of the day in their home on the Dorset coast.

'More tea, Ruby?' Aunt Dee asked her briskly. 'I'm sure Lauren is gasping!'

Aunt Ruby said sourly, 'Not for me, thank you. The last lot never saw a teapot in its life.' Her sharp gaze surveyed me critically, my five-foot-three in flat sandals, my short dark hair nicely styled yesterday at Odette's to frame the face Grant always called 'heart-shaped', the blue-grey eyes he called too 'the windows of a very, very sweet soul . . . '

I could hear him saying it. I could always hear him.

Aunt Ruby was still surveying me. 'Well, Lauren, I really don't know what we're letting ourselves in for, do you? Planes and boats, food packed full of grease and garlic. I should have put my foot down and stayed at home.'

'I'm sure it'll be very nice, Aunt Ruby,' I tried to soothe her, without much success. She was still bemoaning her fate as I started for the serving counter.

'That's Hayden in the queue,' Aunt Dee directed. 'Yes, him with the fair hair and glasses. Those are his kiddies, they're so excited, bless their hearts!'

There was an expressive grunt from Aunt Ruby.

'Didn't you tell me he's some sort of teacher?' I asked mildly.

'Yes, indeed. A clever man, dear. He teaches maths.'

I murmured, 'Ah! That sort of teacher.'

At the counter I loaded a tray in haste to catch up with this stranger who was to be my obligatory travelling companion. He was tall, thin, pale-faced, his light-blue eyes chilly behind strong-lensed spectacles, his serious mouth unready to smile. Yes, he looked every bit a maths teacher.

'Hi, there!' I announced myself. 'I'm Lauren. I believe you're my Aunts' godsend of a neighbour?'

'Hayden Jardine. Good morning.' He turned quickly to the delicate-faced boy of maybe five or six tugging at his arm. '*Not* chocolate, Jamie, don't you know better than that? . . . Nor you, Alicia!'

'That's not fair, is it?' the hunch-shouldered, sulkily frowning girl demanded. 'Just 'cos it's bad for *him* . . . '

She trailed off into rebellious mutter-ings, shrugging in an openly insolent

11

manner. It was a sobering thought — if I needed one — that Alicia Jardine was, so to speak, my 'holiday task'. I sized her up with dismay: a shade taller than me, in a floppy top and jeans and trainers, her long hair straggling untidily. Noticing my interest, she coolly stared me out.

Nearing the pay-desk, I made a new effort to break the ice with her father.

'It's nice you've helped my Aunts out, I do thank you for that! I've been so tied up in London the last few months — '

He said, 'Evidently.' A one-word accusation that set me back on my heels — and he went on to amplify it. 'There were urgent repairs needed to their house. Mrs. Pym was very unwell and Miss Roache hurt her back. They're elderly ladies. They need some support.'

'I know that! But so does my — my friend who's a complete invalid after an accident — and I can't be in two places at once! When I phone every few days, Aunt Dee always says everything's fine — '

'Can you really imagine her admitting everything's not?'

'Oh. Well, no. But — '

He didn't wait for any 'buts', moving off with his tray. The two children followed in gloomy procession.

I muttered, 'Well!' Clearly, the Jardine family weren't exactly happy bunnies. I was frowning myself as I followed on. It was upsetting that Aunt Dee seemed to have kept me in the dark about her problems and turned for help to a stranger.

Back at the table, Tina had located us and was chatting in her easy manner to Aunt Dee, predicting we would all have a wonderful time — a luxury cruise ship, sea and sun, gorgeous things to eat, *who* could ask for more?

Aunt Ruby certainly could, declaring if we weren't all sick on the boat we would suffer sunstroke and insect bites ashore, let alone raging food poisoning. She had packed five packets of Dr. Wright's Special Strength Stomach Powders, but still feared the worst. As for the imminent flight, 'If the good Lord meant us to fly, wouldn't He have given us wings?'

There seemed no good answer to that. Even Hayden Jardine, morosely sipping his black coffee, had no crushing response to hand.

All too soon Tina was saying her farewells, and I walked with her to the exit doors. She asked me, 'You'll keep in touch, won't you? — I'll be dying to know if Dr. Wright's Powders save the day — and I'll pop in on Grant, I promise.'

'Thanks. I hope Elaine makes you more welcome than she does me — she hates seeing me at the door, even though I've come to sit with Grant while she's out. She — she makes me feel like a criminal.'

'You've told me. But the accident *wasn't* your fault — Elaine knows, we all know! Only, you see — she's having to rethink her whole life. You can understand that, you've had to rethink yours. Enjoy this holiday, you'll be well out of all the stress for a little while!'

'You think so? Even with the Jardine mob along? Him especially!'

She made a face. 'He's not bad looking — in an 'if you haven't done your homework, stay in at break' kind of way. Perhaps he'll mellow in the sunshine!'

'Perhaps,' I said without conviction.

We exchanged a wave as she set off back to her car and the London flat that was home. I would gladly have gone with her.

* * *

One of those lined-up aeroplanes with the coloured tails took off into a clear sky. It took us with it.

I wasn't quite sure how Aunt Ruby was manoeuvred into her seat and her safety-belt. She sat rigid as a board, her eyes shut, her hands clasped as though in prayer. It didn't help when one of the smart, smiling stewardesses gave us the usual demo of emergency procedures in all their ominous detail.

In fact, I had quite a fellow feeling for the querulous old lady. She and I both were wishing ourselves far removed from Aunt Dee's well-meant plans.

The Aunts sat together, with an awed Jamie and his father behind, and in front I partnered Alicia. Already I foresaw we would be partners more or less everywhere.

'Well, isn't this exciting?' I encouraged her. We were buoyant above the green patchwork of countryside, but though I had given her the window place she showed no interest. I pressed on, 'Have you ever had a trip like this before, Alicia?'

'No. We don't do holidays.'

'Then this one will be extra special, won't it?'

Her almost pitying glance plainly said, 'I'm not a child, stop trying to jolly me along.' There was indeed something disturbingly unchildlike about her.

It wasn't long before our in-flight breakfasts arrived, and I could hear

Mrs. Pym's pained lament that she couldn't look a yoghurt in its sickly face at this hour — and *didn't* the plane's jutting wing beside her window look insecure? But she had perked up enough to comment in very audible whispers on neighbouring passengers' hair-do's and apparel.

Alicia gave a petulant push to her untouched breakfast tray. It was my turn to shrug my shoulders and leave her to her own cross-grained devices.

Luckily the flight wasn't too long. In a while, impressive grey and white mountains were spread beneath us, and then came a world of blue water with islands basking in bright sunlight. There was a buzz of expectation among the passengers, and a red-haired boy opposite was fairly bouncing in his seat, being admonished by his mother, 'Just calm down, Joey, or you'll send the plane into a spin!' I wished the girl beside me — and her young brother, coughing at intervals all through the flight — would bounce too.

The wheels touched down smoothly. This was Venice, most romantic of cities, conjuring up visions of priceless art treasures, picturesque buildings, graceful gondolas sliding through fairytale canals. For us, at present there were just the airport buildings — and the small matter of capturing our baggage on the carousel.

I shared this scramble with Hayden. 'All good fun!' I said to him. His chilly nod seemed to imply that little things pleased little minds.

After that came a slight hiccup. As we trailed through a security checkpoint, Hayden was beckoned aside for closer scrutiny. Aunt Ruby predicted darkly we would all end up languishing in a foreign jail. I thought Alicia looked distinctly pleased about the incident: Jamie burst into a medley of sobs and coughs, not consoled by Aunt Dee's soothing arms.

'Here's your Daddy again, all safe and sound, darling,' she told him at length, and he flew back to Hayden.

You couldn't really fault the gentle firmness of his father's treatment, calming him down, sorting out some kind of medication.

Before all the preliminaries finally let us board the boat there was a crowded coach ride and a sojourn in a large departure hall, waiting for our group number to be called. People in cheery holiday garb sat around brightly chatting or munching refreshments, or straggled outside for a first glimpse of the boat moored at the quay. When Hayden took Jamie out for some gulps of fresh air, I followed on — and my own first glimpse drew from me a wondering 'Wow!'

'It's HUGE.' Jamie, holding fast to his father's hand, was staring wide-eyed.

'Bigger than huge,' I agreed. 'More like a block of flats than a boat. I wonder how they actually make it move, Jamie!' I looked round at Hayden, who was regarding the towering vision gravely. 'Interesting, yes?'

His succinct 'Very,' didn't indicate much interest. But he actually had more to say. 'Perhaps I should apologise to you, Miss — er . . . Your Aunt did all the bookings and she arranged one cabin for herself and her sister, one for Jamie and me, and you're with Alicia. It wasn't my idea.'

'I'm 'Lauren', please! No, don't worry, it's fine by me,' I said, not quite truthfully. It was only today Aunt Dee had told me this small detail.

'Well, if it's a problem, we'll change things round. Your Aunt thought Jamie would get more rest this way. She's a very caring person.'

'It's no problem,' I insisted. I was watching Alicia, who had followed us and was propped against a railing to stare moodily at the bright scene, the line of passengers filing aboard the massive white vessel with its tiers of balconied cabins, the water blue as the sky above. I whispered tentatively, 'I'm afraid she's not happy about this holiday.'

'Take no notice. And don't stand any nonsense from her.' He had dropped his voice too. 'She — still misses her mother. Quite a lot.'

I murmured, 'Oh. I'm sorry.'

Very thoughtfully I went back inside to report that the 'Bella Italia' was a sight to behold.

When our turn to board did arrive, the first shock was being photographed in a rather drooping group alongside two blonde girls in saucy sailor garb, holding between them a lifebelt banner: '*BENVENUTI A BORDO!*' (One 'Welcome Aboard' picture which wouldn't claim a forefront place in the photoshop!) What followed was like stepping into some super-palatial hotel. One of several busy, shiny lifts bore us way up to the seventh deck, and so finally to find our quarters: down a length of carpeted corridor lined with matching doors, two of our cabins were adjacent and one was some way along. That one had to be mine.

At least the luggage had beaten us to

it. I led the way in.

'Look, Alicia! A balcony with chairs . . . TV, fridge, telephone . . . all these wood panels and pictures . . . nice shower-room through here . . . Right, which bed do you fancy?'

'I don't care. Whatever.'

'Then I'll take this one. We can sort our things out later — we'll need something a bit glam for the Welcome Aboard Dinner . . . ' This flow of enthusiasm was too forced to last long, and I gave up with an expressive sigh. 'Well, you do what you like. I'll just see if the Aunts want help settling in. You do realise they're not so young, and Mrs. Pym has health problems, so they'll appreciate some support from all of us?'

I said it the more shortly as it recalled Hayden Jardine's reproving words to me earlier. Alicia's response, her eyes rolled silently ceilingwards, was a good example of 'dumb insolence'.

I found Aunt Ruby flopped on her bed, clutching her large handbag to her bosom as though it were a lifebelt. She looked tired and bewildered. Aunt Dee was bustling round opening up suitcases.

'How's your room, Laurie?' she enquired. 'I do hope the little boy will be all right, poor lamb. I know Hayden's really worried about him.'

'How do they manage when Hayden's at work?'

'Well, I don't know, because he's only been doing private coaching at home since they moved in next to us — a couple of months ago after the Jacksons went. I believe he left his last post suddenly, just before they came. Now then, Ruby love, *don't* go to sleep or you'll feel worse when you have to wake up!' she coaxed her sister. 'Tell me what you'll wear this evening and I'll hang it up . . . '

She was well in command, as always a walking miracle — borne upon thin sun-tanned legs and pink trainers. I lingered to help a short while, but the thought of my room-mate kicking her heels alone disturbed me.

'Do you mind sharing with that child?' Aunt Dee sounded just a shade guilty, lowering her voice. 'I just hope maybe you can get through to her. Someone has to! She was — er — excluded from her last school. Which means she was thrown out.'

'Oh. Do you know why?'

She shook her head. 'Hayden doesn't like to discuss it. Well, of course he doesn't! But if you can find out, we'll know what we're dealing with, won't we? ... Ruby, how about your navy crepe two-piece with that nice embroidered blouse? ...'

I left them to it. Slowly and thoughtfully, I returned along the passageway.

★   ★   ★

Alicia said, 'A steward man came. A funny little man. He said he's Giuseppe and he'll look after us.'

'That's nice! Would you like to

explore around a bit?'

'I don't care,' was her stock response. But she trailed along with me.

'Exploring around' was an experience. A vast atrium towered to the height of all the decks, with a lavish décor of paintings and statuary. There were bars, cafeterias, restaurants; a whole arcade of different shops, enquiries office, a booking counter for excursions; and finally we found, emerging into the fresh air past a sun-deck refreshments area, a great array of lined up lounge-beds surrounding swimming pools and a Jacuzzi. Far, far below us, the blue sea glistened and sparkled. All around was chatter and movement, people leaning on the rails to point out, in various languages, the Venetian landmarks sliding past.

I was quite amazed that we were already under way. There was no perceptible sense of motion in the massive vessel.

Alicia had plodded around in silence, clearly determined to look bored. But here for a moment I paused, sitting on a vacant sun-bed to tap out a text on my mobile phone.

'For my friend,' I explained. 'I promised to let him know when we got this far. Grant is — he's a permanent invalid, I'm afraid. There was an accident . . . '

It wasn't easy to say even this much. I expected Alicia to respond with her careless shrug, but she didn't.

'You were going to marry him some time ago, weren't you? I heard Miss Roache talking to Mrs. Pym about it.'

'That's right. It didn't work out. But last year we met up again and started working together, and that did work out! I did the piano solos and accompaniments, he did the songs and violin pieces — oh, we were really climbing the ladder!'

'What happened to him?'

'We'd had this really late concert — it was in Cardiff — and we were both exhausted — but he wanted to drive straight back to London on a freezing foggy night because the next day was Elaine's birthday.'

'Who's she?'

'The girl he's engaged to now. Well, I told him he was crazy, we'd go back to London first thing in the morning, but he wouldn't listen. And I let him go, I didn't stop him. I could have hidden the car keys, I could have . . . ' I drew a deep breath. 'We'd had this blazing row. And I just went to bed in the hotel and left him to it. Halfway back he fell asleep at the wheel. The car ran into a barrier . . . '

Why was I telling my impossibly painful tale to a young stranger I didn't know or even much like? Why was I pouring out rending memories of an English winter night, here in this balmy evening glow of Italian sunshine? The girl would be deriding me as an idiot who couldn't keep her emotions decently to herself.

And yet, as her dark eyes lifted to mine, there wasn't contempt or insolence in them. Rather I saw brief interest, even sympathy — and a sudden chilling reflection of my own horror and grief.

'So you don't still do the music thing on your own?'

'No. I never shall again.' I made a fierce effort to get rid of the choking lump in my throat. 'Oh, I've had a few other jobs . . . but mostly I try to help out with Grant, visiting him in the hospital, getting things he needs — as much as Elaine will let me. He'll leave there soon after this big operation he's had. Then they're getting married.'

'Um.' She considered the words seriously. 'I bet you miss the music, don't you?'

'I suppose so. Do you like music?'

'Some,' she said guardedly.

The strange conversation was ended then by the jangle of an answering text message:

'Have fun! Guess what, my electric buggy arrives this week. Say hi to the Aunts. Luv, Grant'

Something made me hold it out for Alicia to read. Again her eyes lifted seriously to mine. She said, 'He sounds cool.'

'Well, we won't be cool if we're late for our first dinner.' I stood up quickly. 'I hope you know the way back to the cabin, I'm not sure I do!'

''Course I know,' was her answer to that.

The depressing sight of luggage still unsorted met us. I began rummaging things out, parking things in drawers. Alicia had found on the TV screen a travel map with a pulsing dot showing the boat's progress, and she slouched on her bed to watch it. Noticeably, she looked really nothing like the father with whom she seemed in a state of permanent warfare. Jamie, of course, did resemble him. (Poor child, I reflected uncharitably.)

'Have you something nice to change into?' I suggested.

'I'm not changing. We're only going to eat, aren't we? Not meet the Queen?'

'True. But you could make a little effort.'

'Well, I haven't got any fancy things. I don't *like* fancy things! Dad said I should bring my school clothes to look decent — can you imagine that? School uniform?'

In fact, I could imagine that quite easily.

'We can do better than that! Look, we're much of a size — borrow something of mine till we can go shopping.'

She flared at me, 'I'm not wearing your stupid things!'

I spread on her bed a white scoop-necked tee-shirt with a swirl of diamante on the front, paired with a plain denim skirt. 'Just try it on while I'm changing. I dare you!'

When I emerged from the shower-room, I expected to find nothing touched. Instead, arrayed in the modest finery, she was surveying herself critically in a mirror.

'That looks okay.' I was careful not to over enthuse. 'Shall we put your hair up?'

'What's wrong with my hair?'

'Nothing. But why not experiment? Live dangerously, eh?'

She glared at me. But surprisingly, she let me brush her long, thick dark hair into an attractive casual knot.

'Shoes?' I hinted. With footwear we were different sizes, but she unearthed from her luggage a pair of blue flipflops. The whole effect was a rather amazing transformation.

I surveyed my handiwork a little smugly. It was a smugness of short duration.

The Aunts were just ready, Aunt Ruby resplendent in navy crepe that strained a little over her ample figure, Aunt Dee beanpole thin in a gipsy skirt and black top. Hayden and Jamie also produced themselves on time, the little boy looking tired and wan. We made quite an impressive group piling into a lift: I hung on tightly to Aunt Ruby, who was clutching her walking stick with a look of grim resignation.

'Ristorante Giordano,' the lift's recorded

commentary announced. A stream of more or less elegant passengers were drifting and dawdling in the same direction. The 'Ristorante', when finally we arrived there, seemed vast: its white-spread tables sparkled with silver and glass, each place with an elaborately folded blue or lilac napkin to match the lamp-shades. Above, a balcony with a gleaming brass rail was set out with still more tables.

Aunt Dee breathed in my ear, 'Whatever have you done to that child? Have you noticed, Hayden can't take his eyes off her?'

I hadn't noticed, but I saw it then as we were escorted to our table. His gaze was far more startled — and sad — than it was admiring.

It was swiftly obvious that our first dinner aboard would prove a disaster. Jamie shrank into his seat with awe at the whole impressive scene, mutely watching the regiments of waiters treading the aisles with shoulder-high pyramids of dishes, until at length his head drooped in fitful sleep. Aunt Ruby frowned her way through the menu and decided there wasn't a single item she could digest — even with the aid of Dr. Wright's Powders, whose bilious-green packet stood on the table as a warning to all of us. Alicia was scarcely better, wanting chips and beans or nothing.

Conversation around our circular table flagged horribly, despite Aunt Dee's brightest efforts. It was Alicia, next to me, who reached across the table to poke Jamie awake and sent flying his untouched glass of fruit juice. An orange flood invaded our pristine tablecloth and trickled into Aunt Ruby's navy crepe lap.

Aunt Dee, fussing with tissues and muttered dear-dears and never-minds, was quickly relieved by our brisk and smiling personal waiter, Eugenio: 'Is okay, Signora, I make all right for you! . . . '

'Alicia.' Hayden's glacial blue eyes had turned to her. 'We'll go upstairs. Now, please!'

She glared back at him, not moving. Aunt Dee said doubtfully, 'Hayden, dear, she's hardly eaten a thing yet — and there's some yummy desserts on the menu — '

'That's too bad. First she has to learn to behave.'

Some impulse made me jump up from my seat.

'Hayden, you stay here with Jamie or he'll get upset. I'll take Alicia up to our cabin, shall I?'

Before he could protest I had taken the girl's arm gently. For a moment she looked at me in mute defiance, but then thankfully she stood up. Aunt Dee flashed me a quick smile.

Back between the lines of tables with their cheerfully eating and drinking and chattering diners, we made our disgraced way. In the lift, I hesitated a moment, and then didn't press the button for our 'home' deck. Alicia asked suspiciously, 'Where are we going?'

'A breath of fresh air would be nice, don't you think?'

The sun-deck had no sun now. Instead, there were strings of coloured lights against a dim sky, the shadowy sea slipping past far below. It was a clear, beautiful Italian evening. Occasional people strolled by, but mostly everyone was busied elsewhere with meals or entertainments. Parts of the deck were being hosed down, ready for a new morning's influx of sun worshippers.

I said gently, 'This is nice. Alicia, if you're hungry I'm sure we can find you something in one of the places. But — '

We had found a couple of seats, and for a few minutes she had sat beside me in moody silence. Ignoring the lack of response, I ploughed on.

'But I want to ask you something. I'd really like an answer. Why are you trying so hard to make your poor Dad unhappy?'

'What's it got to do with you?'

'Not a lot, I suppose! Except we're room-mates, and I hope we'll be friends — and it bothers me. Look, couldn't you just tell him 'sorry' for that fuss at the table just now?'

Her coal-dark eyes, so utterly unlike Hayden's, looked straight into mine.

'I'm not sorry. And — he's *not* my Dad!'

'He's not — ?'

'That's what I said. I'm tired, I want to go to bed — do you mind?'

I should have guessed. Of course I should have guessed. It proved, if proof were needed, my deficiencies as a family counsellor.

Back in the cabin I went on quietly sorting out my things, and within minutes Alicia had extinguished herself in her bed — and, surprisingly, was fast asleep. In repose, her face was a young child's, innocent and peaceful.

There were all sorts of entertainments on offer around the 'Bella Italia' on this first night afloat, but I was scarcely in the mood for any of them. Looking out at the darkened sea, I was thinking of Grant — not the frail and damaged Grant of today, but the man I used to know, a lifetime ago. I could still hear his laughter, for in those days we laughed a lot. I could still feel his warm kiss on my lips.

2

'Hi!' a friendly voice called to me along the passageway lined by cabin doors.

I recognised the mother of Joey, the flame-haired young boy whose excitement had threatened to explode on the flight out. He was just as lively now in the early morning, tugging at her as she stopped to speak to me.

'I fancied another hour in bed,' she was saying, 'but this little monster had other ideas! Don't tell me your kids are still sleeping? — or is your husband coping with them?'

'My — ?' I gulped, seriously shocked. 'He's not my husband! And they're not my children, I'm just helping with them. We — we're rather a complicated party! — '

Her mistake was understandable, but she laughed and apologised. I explained just how complicated our group was, and we exchanged names and a few more pleasantries. Kelly-Ann Baxter was probably around my own age — 'middish twenties' I called them: tall and slim, her hair copper-auburn. She also shared Joey's bubbling enthusiasm.

'I saw you had a little prob at dinner last night, I felt for you! . . . We go ashore at Bari today, don't we? What's Bari got? If it's old buildings, my husband Rob will be taking all his boring photos. Let's hope Joey pals up with your little one, it might keep them both out of mischief! . . . '

I agreed politely, though I wasn't sure Jamie ever got around to mischief. We went on our way with a mutual, 'See you later!'

I found Aunt Dee already up and dressed, stirring around on tiptoe while her sister snored quietly. She welcomed me with her usual warmth, but her discerning eyes were a little too sharp.

'Laurie, you haven't switched into holiday mode yet.'

'I'm trying!' I said honestly.

'Then try harder, my dear. Can I say something to you? — you won't be angry? You've been in touch with Grant already, haven't you?'

I had to mumble assent, feeling my face start to burn.

'Of course you worry about him, we all do. But — you know, is it really helping him — and helping you — to hang on to something that's over? Elaine has turned out a very loyal and courageous young woman, I admire her for standing by him when many would walk away. It's not an easy future she's taking on, nothing like the future she expected. So mightn't it be wise to let them sort their lives out by themselves? — and get back your own life, your gift for music that you've buried away after working so hard all those years? . . . Forgive me for preaching at you, but — I just can't bear to see you so unhappy . . . '

She had hinted at all this before, but never in such plain words. Though her voice was full of concern, I felt as though I had been struck in the face.

Aunt Ruby woke at that moment with a loud grunt, asked the time, and declared she hadn't closed her eyes all night. I took the chance to slip away.

In fact, I was a little angry. Aunt Dee meant so well, but this time she didn't understand. She hadn't been there on the night of the tragic accident to witness the stupid quarrel I had with Grant about getting home for Elaine's birthday, the things we both said before I stamped off up the hotel stairs — and let him drive recklessly away in a daze of resentment and sheer exhaustion . . .

'Alicia, come on!' I called my room-mate's name quite sharply. 'We're all nearly ready for breakfast!'

'Are you?' She rolled over, burying her face in her pillow. 'I'm staying here.'

'You know we'll be going ashore this morning? — This is Italy, and the sun's shining? Okay, fine, stay there and miss all the fun if you want!'

She muttered, '*What* fun?' But when I continued to ignore her, after a few minutes she crawled sulkily out of bed and into the shower. We were both just about ready when a hand tapped on our door.

''Morning,' Hayden greeted me.

I gave a little start of surprise. He did look oddly different in more casual gear with his fair hair breeze-blown. Even more amazing, Jamie had a touch of colour in his face, and smiled at me shyly. They had been exploring, Hayden said. They had ridden twice in the glass lift, and watched the sea from the top deck.

'So you're ready for breakfast,' I applauded. 'Maybe we can beat the crush!'

We didn't beat it. By the time we had collected the Aunts and found a vacant lift, the ship's entire complement of passengers seemed to have crammed themselves into the area of serving counters, drinks dispensers and seating. There was bustle and chatter, an atmosphere of coffee and grilled food, with a relentless amplified background of 'O Sole Mio', 'Santa Lucia', 'Arrivederci Roma,' etc.

By sheer luck Hayden grabbed a table just being vacated. Aunt Ruby, slumping heavily into her chair, said she could face only tea (or what passed for tea) and a tiny piece of toast, if someone would kindly fetch it. She was sorry to be a nuisance to us all. She would have been far better off left at home.

'You're no trouble,' Aunt Dee assured her. 'But do try to eat! — you must keep your strength up for the shore trip, dear.'

'You can all go on the trip. I've lived enough years without seeing this place, so I daresay I can live some more. I'd only be a burden to you.'

Unusually, Aunt Dee looked upset and anxious. It was Hayden who said soothingly, 'Don't worry, Mrs. Pym, we'll find you something to eat and then you'll feel better.' He nodded to Alicia to sit next to Jamie, and then made a somewhat imperious gesture to me across the table. I jumped up, feeling like the class dunce summoned to solve an impossible problem on the blackboard.

Together we queued with trays and braved the scramble for drinks — a hazardous process with a human octopus of jostling elbows and arms intruding as you tried to position a light plastic cup under a squirting spout. Hayden muttered, 'You'd think everyone had been on a fast for six months.'

He was squinting closely at the directions beside the tea machine — which were listed, like every notice, in assorted languages. I pointed out, 'Did you know you've picked up the herbal tea bags? I'm not sure whether Aunt Ruby — '

He muttered again, impatiently, not very politely.

Back at the table we handed out platefuls. For the children there were austere bowls of porridge: Jamie's was received with resignation, Alicia's with abject disgust — not helped by Aunt

Ruby's comment, 'I don't reckon that's real porridge . . . now my mother made it every morning in a big pan — you remember, Dee, it really lined your ribs to start the day! . . . '

The trials of our first breakfast weren't too far short of last night's first dinner. I wasn't even sure what I ate — or if I ate. Aunt Dee raced back to the cabins for her sister's forgotten tablets.

The day's shore excursion had been booked for everyone, but it seemed Aunt Dee had decided to stay on board with Ruby: 'I'll see she has a nice rest, all the travelling yesterday just wore the poor soul out,' she muttered to me. I offered to stay behind in her stead, but she wouldn't hear of it.

Which meant that around eleven o'clock, when the boat had docked, I lined up — in the impressive theatre, with curtained stage and ranks of seats — alongside the Jardine family, to be issued with our luminous orange identity stickers and instructions for disembarking. It struck me our party stood out in the crowd as exhibiting the least '*joi de vivre*.' The Jardines inevitably carried their own gloomy cloud around with them.

In our turn we filed past the control check (where luckily Hayden wasn't mistaken for a secret agent), off the ship and on to the soil of Italy. It was truly a glorious day, the sky cloudless, the warmth of the sunshine very strong. A group of coaches stood ready to ferry us the short distance into the town.

As for seeing the sights, we weren't too fortunate with our guide for the on-foot tour, a pleasant young lady but so quietly voiced and strongly accented as to be more or less unintelligible. It was just as well Aunt Ruby had declined the hot cobblestone streets of the old parts of town, where close buildings basked in the sun, lines of washing and bedding thrust through windows sought the air. Jamie was soon lagging miserably. Alicia plodded grimly in the rear in her heavy trainers and an unnecessary jacket.

In the circumstances, the Basilica of San Nicola and the Church of San Gregorio largely left us unmoved. The walls of the Norman Castle were memorable mainly for a glimpse of Kelly-Ann and Joey waving to us at a distance while a tall man with several cameras strung about him was lining up a picture. So Rob's 'boring old photos' had materialised!

We ended up on the busy coast road, relieved by a spread of grass and numerous picturesque palm trees, with a view across blue water and flotillas of gently moving boats. Jamie flopped down in the shade. It seemed a long wait before we could join the first coach back to the ship.

Somehow in the scramble aboard we were split up, Jamie and Alicia near the front, Hayden and I a few rows back. I noticed the sun had reddened Hayden's face, particularly his rather bony nose. It hadn't cured his lack of companionable small talk.

Well, it was ridiculous to sit here in chilly silence! I decided a few point blank questions might be helpful for the future.

'Hayden, while we've a moment here . . . Alicia and I are getting along nicely, but I do feel I'd understand her better if I knew more about her problems. I believe she had — er — troubles at her last school?'

'In other words, why was she obliged to leave.'

'Well, yes. It must have been something serious?'

'It was,' he said unhelpfully.

'Like — ?'

'Like something serious. As I just said.'

I drew a deep breath, and then threw caution to the winds.

'But there's something else bothering her. She told me last night you're not really her Dad?'

'That's right.'

'So she's an adopted child?'

'I adopted her when I married Nancy

— her mother. She lost her father a while back.'

'That's sad. And now her mother has died too, so she has only — '

I pulled up the injudicious words short, but he finished them for me. 'Only me. Correct. Is there anything else you want to know?'

The rather impossible moment was saved by someone's shopping falling from the rack above us in a snowstorm of carrier bags.

Back at the ship, its vast size reared up like a towering white mountain-face gleaming in the sun, we trooped aboard. I was quite glad to be back — even to face another meal.

⋆ ⋆ ⋆

Every cabin was provided daily with a booklet setting out all the activities available on board and ashore on that date. Over lunch I flipped through it and read out possibilities.

Aunt Ruby was looking better for a

morning's sleep, and Aunt Dee seemed happier. The six of us found something in the lavishly spread-out buffet that we could eat — Alicia bearing to her place a dish piled with about eight slices of pizza. Aunt Ruby quite mildly told her she would clog up her digestive system. Hayden, for a wonder, didn't comment.

In fact, the pizza was delectable. I could have eaten eight slices myself.

The sun-deck was crammed with scantily-clad baking bodies prone on the rows of lounge beds, just occasionally stirring to oil themselves or each other: a spectacle of '*La Dolce Vita*' personified. But spaces were free in a shaded area of tables and seats near a counter serving ice-cream and drinks. We parked Aunt Ruby there, beneath a large straw hat and an enveloping stole, to eye grimly the gorgeously tanned (or lobster-reddened) people strolling by for refreshments.

'A dip in the pool, anyone?' I enquired. 'Or card games, or an aerobics session — or the library, or the shops?'

'In the pool, please.' Jamie spoke up surprisingly.

'Can he?' I asked Hayden.

'The water's good for him. But give it another half hour after eating.'

We went below to sort out our swimming gear. I had brought along a plain black bikini, brief but stylish — which doubtless would earn comments from Aunt Ruby. Alicia flatly declined to join in, and Aunt Dee murmured to me, 'I'd love to another time, but I'll stay with Ruby while she's still settling down.'

So it was Jamie, Hayden and I who presently sampled the biggest pool. Blue-tiled in a dazzle of blazing sun, it was well tenanted, with young children splashing and shouting in the shallows. I watched Hayden plant two precisely folded towels on the surround and set down his glasses on top. Without them his face looked startlingly younger — especially with its prominently sunburnt nose: not a handsome face, but the features were regular enough, the eyes palely glacial, the mouth that so rarely smiled. I supposed it wasn't his fault that he still looked like a maths master dragooned into supervising Form 4 at the local baths.

There was no space for serious swimming, but it didn't matter, especially as Joey's family arrived and Joey had a blow-up beach ball. I couldn't quite believe Hayden and Jamie and I, with an exuberant Joey and Kelly-Ann (in vivid pink swimwear even briefer than mine) were playing 'catch' with much splashing and a few impromptu duckings. It was a delight to see Jamie transformed from a sad and suffering waif into a riotous small boy.

In fact, it was Hayden who seemed to be in some way suffering, squinting painfully in the glare, trying to clear splashes from his face. But the interlude ended abruptly when Jamie slipped over backwards under the water. Kelly-Ann snatched him to his feet, but he coughed and choked for several minutes.

'I'll see to him.' Hayden grabbed up clothes and towels. On no occasion could you fault his care of the frail little boy. 'Lauren, would you look after the rest of our things? — bring them down when you're ready?'

'Of course,' I agreed.

Kelly-Ann watched beside me the father and son merge into the throng of people. She said, 'Poor little kid. Well, at least your boyfriend's game for a laugh! — my Rob's off photographing obscure bits of ship!'

I amended, 'He's not my — '

'Oh yes, you said. Right, I'd better sort out Joey.'

As she drifted away, I sat on the lounger where our possessions were parked to dab away excess water. Before I was through, I was startled by a mobile phone trilling beside me. The very sedate ringtone wasn't mine. It came from among Hayden's left-overs.

Instinctively, I answered the call: 'Sorry, Mr. Jardine's not here — can I give him a message?'

'Who is this?' a girl's voice asked.

'I'm a — a friend. We're away on holiday — '

'Oh, you must be — is it Laura?'

'Lauren. Lauren Roache.'

'I'm Megan Howell, I'm Denny's sister. Hi!' (I was a little dazed by that rather unlikely 'Denny'.) 'You haven't heard of me? — he's a secretive so-and-so! . . . I just called to see how he's getting on. He deserves a good time, doesn't he?'

'Well — ' I floundered, still more dazed. 'I'm sorry, I don't know him awfully well yet. My Aunt arranged the holiday for us all, and — '

'Oh yes, the old ladies he's taken under his wing — as though he hasn't troubles enough of his own! Are his eyes bothering him much?'

'His *eyes*?'

'Hasn't he mentioned that either?' Her bright, quick manner — about as far removed from Hayden's as any could be — had sobered. 'He got involved in this incident at a petrol station — trust him to be in the wrong place at the wrong time. Young louts they were, trying to rob the place, and vicious with it. He had Jamie with him, he was terrified for the kid — when one of the young villains made a move towards them he just waded in with a rugby tackle. Can you imagine that? — '

I muttered a deeply shocked, 'Good grief!'

'Denny got sprayed in the face with a chemical. It nearly blinded him. Well, he got some sort of bravery award — a lot of use when it's cost you most of your sight, and what you've got left isn't very stable. And the robbers got clean away. That's the story, but *don't* let on I've told you, he goes ballistic about my big mouth!'

'I'm glad you told me. It explains . . .' I tailed off, still hardly able to comprehend this extraordinary tale. For a very quiet man, Hayden Jardine seemed to have led a far from quiet life.

His sister was saying it was nice to talk to me, maybe we would meet sometime — 'And do enjoy your holiday, the brochure I saw made it sound wonderful. An enchanted voyage! ...'

Then she had gone. Still utterly dumfounded, I put down the phone and started wriggling damply into some clothes.

Alicia, who had been watching from a distance, was mooching across to ask, 'Who was that ringing Dad's phone?'

'His sister. Just to ask how we're all doing.'

'Auntie Megan.' She pulled a face. 'Did you tell her it's mega-boring?'

'No, I didn't. Because it isn't! How about an ice?'

'Don't mind,' she conceded.

'Let's see if the Aunts want one.'

We went back to the shaded area. Aunt Dee, after probably a disrupted night, had dozed off in the warmth with her chin on her chest. Aunt Ruby, slumped beside her, had her eyes tight shut and her mouth hanging open. Below in the cabins, Jamie was probably still choking.

'Great!' Alicia muttered, as though summing up the whole scenario.

I wondered wryly what she would think of her Auntie Megan's so imaginative phrase, 'an enchanted voyage'.

★   ★   ★

'Lifeboat drill?' I groaned.

''Fraid so,' Aunt Dee confirmed. 'I daresay it won't take long.'

When we all gathered presently for afternoon 'tea and cakes', Hayden called the matter to mind, as though giving warning of an after-class detention. Not that it was necessary to remind us. The loudspeakers had already repeated 'an important announcement for all passengers' — in the inevitable succession of Italian, German, French, etc. Shortly the alarm would sound, everyone must attend their appointed muster stations wearing those brightly-hued lifejackets stored in the cabins.

Only Alicia looked vaguely interested

that something — anything! — was about to happen. We awaited the signal in our cabin, and I was still turning over and over in my mind that strange phone-call, and wondering whether to speak to her about the petrol station 'hold-up'. Surely it should have inspired in her more admiration and respect for Hayden? But this really wasn't the right moment for complex discussion.

She actually giggled a little over the business of getting into the bulky orange life-preservers, and at the stream of similarly clad passengers hurrying along. Soft-voiced and smiling Giuseppe was on hand to make sure all was in order.

Inevitably, Aunt Ruby wasn't happy. She couldn't hurry for anyone, she said, and how was a body supposed to breathe with this orange monstrosity strapped to one's chest? Hayden was occupied fully with a frightened Jamie who was unconvinced that the 'Bella Italia' wasn't actually foundering — and now I understood the little boy's frequent terrors rather more.

When we eventually lined up on deck in our vividly luminous rows to watch a demonstration of survival techniques, it seemed cruel of the ship's photographer to dart to and fro clicking busily. Not a pretty sight, I was sure.

With the exercise over at last, Aunt Ruby needed a lie-down and Jamie was shedding tears. Alicia heaved a long sigh, flapping over the daily programme back in our cabin. I asked, 'There must be something in this whole huge boat you'd like to see or do?'

'Yes. There's a concert, it's just starting.'

I took the booklet from her, and my heart sank. 'Oh. A piano recital.'

'It's in 'The Studio' — I know where that is. You don't have to come.'

'Oh,' I muttered again. Of all things I really didn't want, it was this — to bring back those lost days with Grant. But I was reluctant to let Alicia wander off alone.

'I'll come! We'll just look in for a few minutes — it may not be any good.'

She knew exactly where to go, though I hadn't taken much notice when we were exploring earlier. The place was smaller than the impressive main theatre, much more intimate: semi-circular lines of plush claret-coloured seats surrounded an uncurtained stage, where flower-decked urns on pillars guarded the gleaming grand piano.

The performance had already begun. As we went in, an attendant handed us slim programmes. Very familiar Mendelssohn was gentle and tender.

I stared hard at the printed page before I could bring myself to look up at the stage. *CLASSICAL PIANO INTER-LUDE — CEDRIC RAPHAEL* was the heading, with a shadowy photograph of the pianist. I raised my eyes at last from the paper version to the flesh and blood performer at the piano.

He was young, certainly not far past thirty: a slimly built man with a sensi-tive, straight-featured face at present full of deep concentration. His light-brown hair, thick and curly, glinted gold under the lights. His hands, at once strong and delicate, travelled easily over the keys — and created magic.

'Mm. Not bad,' Alicia whispered judicially. 'Let's shift into the front!'

In the pause between items she made a dive to change places, and I scrambled after her. Something else I didn't want to do, because now I could follow every note that was played, each finger that played it. And the playing was beautiful! Only, for me, beauty and pain were all one.

Every piece I had played myself, all of them I knew and lived and loved. So short a while ago this had been my world. Mine and Grant's together . . .

I was battling to keep the tears from my eyes, but they wouldn't be held back. The Recital wasn't long, its highlight the soul-stirring 'Revolutionary Prelude' — which did impress the somewhat sparse and inattentive audience. Then, the encore was more Chopin, a Nocturne to tug the heartstrings. My own very last encore on that very last fateful day.

'Are you okay?' Alicia was whispering. I saw her face through a haze, and there was real concern in it. For a moment I couldn't answer her. 'Sit there till you feel better, Lauren. I'm just going to get his autograph.'

Through that enveloping mist I watched her trot up the steps to the stage, where the pianist had lingered to talk to an elderly couple. The audience were drifting away, taking their sacrilege of drinks cans and sweet bags with them. I saw Alicia wait her turn and then hold out her programme to be signed: not just that, but she was chattering as she seldom did, waving her hands about. To my dismay, one of the gestures was towards me.

Both of them, the man and the girl, came down from the stage and straight to my seat. I was aware of gentle, brown-velvet eyes studying my face. A softly accented voice spoke to me.

'Hello. I'm sorry you are not well. You're the young lady's sister, maybe? — '

'Oh no, I — I'm just her friend . . . '
I scrubbed angrily at my blotched face.
'And I'm not ill! I loved your playing,
I'm sorry I'm behaving like an idiot . . . '

'No, no! The music can do this. And
you're a musician too, but you don't
play any more?'

I mumbled some sort of agreement,
aware now what Alicia had been
chattering about. He bent closer, one
of those expressive hands gesturing
towards the bulk of the piano gleaming
down at us.

'That's sad. That isn't good. But you
could play now, while the music is in
your heart. Just for me, the people have
all gone. Please?'

'I'm sorry. I can't. I can't!'

'Go on, give it a go.' Alicia nudged
me in the ribs. 'I would, if I had a
chance! The piano at home is always
locked since I stopped having lessons.'

He answered that broad hint by
granting her 'five minutes, Alicia — no
more — and *pianissimo*!' Waving away
the attendants waiting to clear up, he

sat down next to me. I was quite amazed that Alicia plumped herself down, shook back her hair, and played — with some stumbles but reverently — another so familiar fragment of Chopin.

It actually started my eyes filling again. This whole situation was getting completely out of hand. I wanted just to be away from here, somewhere by myself so I could weep until the tears ran dry.

But evidently that wasn't to be. When Alicia came triumphantly back to us and our genuine applause, she had more personal information to pour out.

'Sorry I messed it up a bit, I'm awfully out of practice. My Dad doesn't like me playing, you see. This is Lauren Roache — she's quite famous, haven't you heard of her? — her Aunt brought us on this holiday, a bit boring really . . . '

'But not my part of it, I hope.' He smiled at her, a gentle, appealing smile. 'Perhaps you would both like a drink?

Come, I'll show you a quiet place. Come, Lauren. Come, Alicia.'

He had our names sorted, and a guiding hand was on my elbow as he ushered us through the doorway and into a neighbouring bar area. He indicated a quiet alcove. Here the décor was all sea and sea-creatures, gilded starfish and silvery dolphins, dark seaweed against turquoise-blue oceans. The lamp on our table was formed like an iridescent shell. Perhaps, in this dimmed lighting, the blotchiness of my face wouldn't show too much? . . .

Though I requested coffee, I was given wine, and Alicia had Coke and some peanuts. She summed up every-thing as 'Cool!'

Somehow, then, we were all talking, reminiscing, and regretting. It was the strangest thing. This man I didn't remotely know, except for the spell of his music, sat there near to me and spread all around some irresistible magic, loosening tongues, opening up closed doors.

Alicia was first, abandoning her usual sulky monosyllables to pour out an impassioned tale about the stopped music lessons: because of 'something a bit awful' that happened at school, so that she never went back there, and her father gave up his teaching job there — 'or they made him give it up,' she hinted darkly. 'He was livid. He still is. And he sold the house, and we moved miles away.' She made it sound like a huge nightmare. A continuing nightmare while the piano stayed locked and father and daughter stayed sadly estranged.

Cedric Raphael's story, in his quiet accented voice, described his childhood home in a pretty Swiss village where his parents ran a small guest-house. He won a place at the Zurich Academy, but for several years he battled against poor health that almost finished his career in music before it began. Against all the odds he had weathered the bad times. Though international concert halls and high acclaim probably would never happen, for the present he had employment he loved on the cruise ships. This, not too demanding, he could cope with and enjoy.

'So no despairing!' he encouraged Alicia. 'What is the saying you have? — the black clouds have bright linings? So your father will forgive you, yes?'

'No chance!' she said flatly. 'You don't know him! Can I get some crisps?'

As she wandered off, a forlorn figure dawdling to survey the sea-life surroundings, he and I were left alone in our corner. Rather awkwardly I looked up from my Recital programme on the table to the man who was watching me with those warm brown eyes.

'It — it's kind of you to bother about her, Mr. — er — '

'Cedric. Please! It's no bother, she seems such a sad young girl. And I'm afraid you're sad too. When I played the Nocturne — '

'That's because it was my very last encore! You see — oh, everything had been like a dream, and then . . . that awful day . . .'

It was unthinkable to describe such intensely private emotions to a stranger. Yet he seemed no stranger, so deeply understanding, his gentle comments so full of sympathy. When my words trailed off, those unquenchable tears were flowing again — but now they were almost tears of relief, quiet and comforting.

Alicia was drifting back to us, and the spell was broken. But I felt my hand held briefly between two consoling hands as he whispered, 'We'll talk again about our troubles! — very soon?'

I whispered back, 'Yes, please.' What other answer could I give?

By now it was high time to be moving on, and I got to my feet. Cedric was telling Alicia he would be playing tonight in the theatre show, and he hoped she would be there. She nodded quite enthusiastically.

As we went in search of the others, she made another of her judicial statements: 'He's sort of nice.'

'Sort of nice,' I echoed.

We found everyone in the Aunts' cabin,

where Aunt Ruby was lying down and everybody else was searching for a mislaid bottle of daily tablets. There was quite a scramble of opening drawers and searching bags. It was actually Alicia, delving in the dressing-table fixture, who produced a phial of pills and asked brightly, 'Are these them, Mrs. Pym?'

They were them. One more panic resolved! . . . or so I thought then.

Before we prepared for dinner I went with Alicia to the shopping arcade. She had some money — 'from Auntie Megan,' she explained. I stood by while she selected a black top with a sparkly *Buon giorno!* across the front, some trousers and a black velvet hair-scrunchie. In fact, I had to supplement Megan's largesse.

'I'll pay you back,' Alicia said gruffly.

'I don't want paying back. I want you to have something you like.'

She muttered something about paying me back anyhow.

It wasn't easy to concentrate on

sorting my own wardrobe while Alicia was showering. In some way I had been living in an ethereal glow ever since she first dragged me into The Studio. It was beyond explaining. I kept seeing again and again a stranger's smile, wondering if he really meant his promise to meet again . . . and whether, that time, I could manage to look rather less of a tear-sodden wreck? . . .

'Laurie, dear!' It was a rather anxious Aunt Dee at the door. 'Sorry to disturb you — but when you helped look for Ruby's medicine, you didn't see her gold locket hiding away somewhere?'

'No. You mean the engraved heart-shaped one?'

'That's it. I'm certain she brought it — and you know how she treasures it because our Mum left it to her. Oh dear, she's so forgetful these days! . . . ' She trailed off with a forced laugh. 'It's probably sitting there grinning at us, right under our noses!'

'I'm sure it will turn up,' I said soothingly. 'Don't worry, Aunt Dee.

We'll be ready in ten minutes, is that all right?'

'That's fine,' she nodded. 'So will we.'

I watched her small figure hurry off along the corridor. My glow had faded just a little. I even found myself shivering with a vague chill of foreboding.

Alicia, emerging from the shower-room, asked casually, 'Who were you talking to?'

'Just Aunt Dee. Alicia, when we were looking for those lost tablets, you didn't notice a gold locket in any of the drawers?'

'A locket?'

'A gold heart on a chain. Very pretty. Did you see it?'

She shook her head. 'Why?'

She was looking me straight in the face, those dark unchildlike eyes of hers coolly inscrutable. I said quietly, 'It seems to have gone missing. Aunt Ruby is very upset.'

'Tough!' Her eyes didn't waver. 'She's a bit ga-ga, isn't she? Can I borrow your hairspray?'

3

The dinner menu didn't fail to provide problems. '*Calamari fritti*', translated as 'fried squid', for once united Alicia and Aunt Ruby in their verdict: my Aunt's 'Disgusting!' and Alicia's 'Gross!' Jamie was actually interested enough to ask, 'If they're sort of octopuses, do they still have all their arms on?' The further mention of '*funghi*', almost had Mrs. Pym reaching for her 'Dr. Wright's' on the spot.

At least tonight nothing was spectacularly spilled, which had to be an improvement. I exchanged a 'thumbs up' with Kelly-Ann across the vast dining area.

Afterwards came a lavish, noisy, colourful Extravaganza in the big theatre, not really to my taste — except for the intermission, when Cedric Raphael played a selection of show tunes. For that, I sat enthralled.

The Aunts had taken charge of a sleepy Jamie so that Hayden could accompany Alicia and me to the theatre. Throughout, he looked supremely bored, and also pained: thanks to my secret confidante Megan, I noticed him flinch at the bright stage lights.

Afterwards, very carefully he lifted the still sleeping little boy back to their own cabin. While Alicia flicked through the TV channels, I seized the chance of a quiet word with Aunt Dee.

'I've some news. Important!' I sat next to her on her bed. 'About Hayden, you're not going to believe it . . . '

The garage hold-up incident sounded all the more unlikely here in these quiet pleasant surroundings. I related all I knew, not much but enough to shock Delia Roache as much as it had shocked me.

'He actually charged in physically to stop those ruffians?' she marvelled. 'How many were there?'

'Enough, I suppose! The thing is, his

eyes were damaged. Quite badly . . . '

She tut-tutted in a horrified way. 'He's never breathed a single word to us! Of course, between you and me, he's not easy to talk to. A bit of a cold fish, poor love . . . And little Jamie saw it all? — no wonder he's afraid of his own shadow, and so upset to be parted from his Daddy!'

'Aunt Dee, do you know where they lived before they moved next to you?'

'North London somewhere. Why?'

'Alicia said 'something awful' happened at her school. Did you know Hayden actually taught there? — it sounded like they both had to leave double quick. If I knew which school it was — '

'St. Luke's,' Aunt Ruby said gruffly from her pillow. We had supposed she was asleep. 'I asked him once.'

'Oh! Ruby, I asked too, I thought he said St. Mark's,' Aunt Dee mused.

I laughed, though I didn't feel like laughing. 'Or St. Matthew's or St. John's? Well, I'll get Tina on the case, she's a whale on research. I'll text her. It's hard to help people when you don't know the background.'

As I left, in the doorway I whispered to Aunt Dee, 'No joy with the locket?' She shook her head. I wondered if she was thinking what I was trying not to think.

The message to my cousin was top priority, and I sent it right away. She answered promptly, 'You must be joking!' But Tina loved a challenge. I had every faith in her.

Though I hadn't said much to Aunt Dee about the earlier piano recital — just that Alicia liked it and the pianist was 'quite good' — it was Cedric Raphael, his music, his gentle kindness, that kept surfacing in my mind that night, even above the troubles of the Jardine family, even — yes, it was true — above my remembrance of Grant. I counted the passing hours, while the huge ship moved smoothly on through the summer darkness.

The next port of call for us, on a blazing day of blue water and blue sky, was Greece. We were due at Katakolon, to visit the site of the very first Olympic Games: probably of interest to many, but my own feeling was 'take it or leave it'.

However, we were taking it. The problem was, our daily Newsletter warned, 'rough walking at the site, wear sensible shoes'.

'I'll be all right here till you get back,' Aunt Ruby insisted at breakfast. 'Dee, you're not to stay with me! It's ridiculous, you travelling all this way and not seeing anything!'

It was Hayden who solved the quandary, taking Giuseppe aside for a quiet word. Our obliging cabin attendant would look in on Mrs. Pym, and arrange for her to be served with light refreshments.

So this time, five of us went through the 'leaving the boat' routine and boarded a waiting motor coach. It was nice to be with Aunt Dee again. I made sure to sit with her, letting the Jardines arrange themselves as they chose.

It seemed a quiet place, the pleasant waterfront contrasting with the looming presence of the 'Bella Italia'. The ride was picturesque and interesting: we kept exclaiming, 'Are those olive trees?' — or, 'Look, oranges growing!' — or 'What a gorgeous garden with that little white house!' I would gladly have sat there longer enjoying the passing countryside basking in the sun. But before long we had reached a parking place thronged with other coaches, groups of tourists, busy guides with clipboards.

Our own guide — Christos, a pleasant man with silvered hair and beard and sun-bronzed skin — proved a godsend. Even my flagging interest was stimulated by his account of the facts and myths of the Ancients. We tramped in the baking heat around the excavations, impressively dating back to 776 BC: we viewed the ruins of temples built to Zeus and Hera, and other names unfamiliar to me: we saw the strip where the very first foot races were held, and read inscriptions marking time-worn masonry or stunted pillars.

Quite early on, Hayden announced he and Jamie would wait in a patch of shade till we returned. Aunt Dee asked in concern, 'Are you all right, dear?'

He answered her shortly, 'I'm fine, thank you! But Jamie's getting too hot and breathless. Anyway, he doesn't understand what all this is about.'

Aunt Dee gave me a knowing look as we moved on. Though Hayden had added clip-on 'shades' to his glasses (not the height of fashion) he was obviously having trouble with the glare of sun and stone.

Alicia's face betrayed a quandary whether to stay with her family or tag along with us. It seemed we were the lesser of two evils. Her presence meant, of course, we couldn't discuss what was in our minds.

Back near the coach, we bought cold drinks from a kiosk, and Olympic souvenir pens. The sun went on blazing. Aunt Dee said her feet resembled balloons.

Returning through the drowsing countryside, we came again to the sea-front. There was a little time to see the local shops with their stands of postcards, tee-shirts and shady hats. The café tables by the water looked tempting, adorned with blue awnings and sunshades, but we were due back on board for a late lunch with Aunt Ruby.

In fact, we found her looking quite bright, and in her cabin a tray bearing the remains of tea and sandwiches, and a little pot of fresh flowers. 'That Giuseppe treated me like a queen,' she told us. 'Dee, do you know, he actually reminded me of — '

'That's nice, dear!' Aunt Dee cut her short, looking strangely flustered. 'All right, let's get ready for lunch — I'm sure you young folks are starving!'

We young folks weren't particularly, but we scattered to freshen up. While

Alicia dragged a comb through her hair and I rummaged out a cool strappy top, she asked out of the blue, 'Why are your Aunts so *old*?'

'Ah, there's a story to that. My Dad's first wife died, you see, he married again — he was quite a bit older than my Mum. And he was the Aunts' 'little brother'.'

'But he was your real Dad.'

'Yes, he was.' I saw now her train of thought. 'Alicia, it must be hard for you, losing people you love, accepting someone who isn't really family. But I'm quite sure Hayden wants to do his best for you and Jamie.'

She asked rather offensively, 'What planet are you on?'

'This one! And I wish you'd believe what I just said. Couldn't you try to meet him halfway?' I stood up briskly. 'Come on, before all the pizzas go!'

On the way, she asked something entirely different.

'That pianist is playing again. 'Tea-time Entertainment', the timetable says.

Did you know?'

'Yes,' I said quietly. 'I did know.'

The knowledge would have lent wings to my feet around even hotter and hoarier sites than that of the First Olympics.

★   ★   ★

Our lifeboat drill pictures, on display in the Photo-shop, were as bad as I had feared. We also discovered two table-tennis tables set up in the fresh air, and joined up with Kelly-Ann to play doubles. While Hayden and Aunt Ruby sat watching, I overheard her lecturing him severely for getting his slightly prominent nose so sunburnt.

A little unfair, I thought. He could scarcely remove it and park it in his pocket. He listened to her gloomily but patiently. When Kelly-Ann called out, 'Take my place here, Hayden?' he shook his head. I wondered, how clearly could he see a small white ball in the dazzling light?

The 'Teatime Entertainment' was getting ever closer. I checked my watch a dozen times. But when the hour arrived, I hadn't bargained on everyone else opting to attend what seemed absurdly like a personal occasion. We all trooped off to The Studio, where light refreshments were available and the mute piano on the platform awaited the magician who could make it speak.

We were in the front, only a few feet away. I watched him come in, and test the height of the stool, and flex his fingers. When he turned to the audience, the warm brown of his eyes looked straight into mine. His smile, that sweet, kind smile, was for me alone.

If I sat there zombie-like, totally spellbound, how could I help that? If people came and went, slurped their tea or chomped their cakes and cookies, I was oblivious to it all. Today I didn't weep, for there was joy in his music and it reached out to me. Joy, too, purely in watching him, the lights turning his hair to gold, highlighting his absorbed face.

When it was over, Alicia cheekily waved to him, and he waved back. Again, his smile was just for me. I didn't even join in the applause. There was no need. He knew what I felt.

Aunt Ruby actually said, 'Well, that was nice. Very nice!'

'He's brilliant.' Alicia was for once enthusiastic. 'He's Swiss, you know. He was ill but he got better. He told us about it yesterday, and he bought us drinks — didn't he, Lauren? If we hang about, do you think he will again?'

I muttered, 'Really, you can't expect . . .' I dreaded she would describe how upset I was yesterday, how he had comforted me. But she didn't. Perhaps she did have some sensitivity.

As everyone was leaving, the two of us did 'hang about' — while I searched under my seat for something I hadn't dropped. And then he was there beside us, his quiet voice asking, 'How are you, Lauren? . . . Alicia you liked the music? You don't like better the modern kind most young people like?'

'Some. But you play what my Mum played. Can I have a go on the piano?'

'Five minutes. *Pianissimo!*' he told her, as he had yesterday.

Sitting beside him, I wasn't aware what Alicia did, only of his presence so near as he asked again how I was feeling today. 'Better,' I said. Indeed, at this moment I was better.

We talked only a little, mostly about music. I told him where we went today, the plans for tomorrow. None of it was very special.

When Alicia drifted back to us, she asked shamelessly, 'Cedric, can we go to that nice place with all the fishes again?'

'So sorry, I have no time just now. Tomorrow we'll meet there,' he promised.

In parting, he touched my arm, he whispered, 'Stay better! — please?'

'I'll try,' I whispered back.

The aftermath of that interlude was odd. I found myself alone with Aunt

Ruby in her cabin, after she sent her sister next door to Hayden and Jamie on some pretext. We were preparing for dinner, and I helped the old lady into a dress that strained uneasily at its seams.

'Lauren,' she shot at me abruptly, 'that young What's-his-name is a very attractive young man!'

She obviously didn't mean Hayden. But I stammered, 'Who do you mean?'

'The piano player. Don't tell me you haven't noticed. I was watching you during that little concert — and you waited afterwards to talk to him?'

'Well. Yes.' I felt my face flushing.

'Stop fiddling with that zipper, if it won't meet it won't meet. Sit down, I've a story to tell you!'

I sat on her bed and she plumped down beside me. I had no idea what was coming.

'You know, I wasn't always an overweight, crotchety old woman! As a girl I was considered quite a beauty. I wanted very much to be an artist, I had some talent — but my old Dad was very strict, he used to say, 'You're an innocent young girl, I won't have you mixing with Bohemian riffraff!' Well, at an exhibition I met an artist who was just making a name for himself. I don't mind saying, I fell for him. Head over heels I did!'

Was it really Aunt Ruby relating this tale? My face probably betrayed blank amazement.

'Mario Amato was — oh, a charmer with the smile of an angel. Your Aunt Dee will tell you. I posed for him secretly, and he gave me a miniature portrait . . . I wore a long white gown and held a sheaf of ruby-coloured roses . . . When he went back home to Italy I was just about to follow him — but my poor Mum was ill, I had to delay — and Mario moved around, and time went on, and we lost touch. A bit later I married my Tom, God rest his dear soul. I've never regretted it for a day. We had a very long and happy marriage . . . '

I thought there was a mist in her dark

eyes. Beautiful eyes they would have been in a young girl's beautiful face. I could see it now as I looked at her.

I asked softly, 'And you never saw Mario again?'

'I never did. But years after, I still liked visiting the exhibitions sometimes — and I found a recent painting of his. It was me, Lauren, in my long white dress, sitting in a garden full of red roses. So he hadn't forgotten me. My Tom wanted to buy it for me, but we didn't have that sort of money.'

I laid a warm hand on her arm, and she didn't shake it off. She gave a rasping cough.

'So that's the story. I don't usually talk about it. But you've had a rough time lately, and I thought — '

Whatever she had thought stayed unspoken. The door opened, and Aunt Dee was asking, 'Are we nearly ready to go down? Here's your face-cream back, Ruby, I did offer it to Hayden but he's rubbing something already on his nose.'

'Is he!' Aunt Ruby grunted. 'Then

it's not working, is it? He'll look like a red traffic light by the time we get home.'

As I took the chance to slip away, I barely suppressed a fit of laughter. I was just as near to tears.

I knew why Aunt Ruby had told me her unlikely fairytale. Only, her so well meant advice was scarcely needed — for Cedric Raphael was no exotic artist painting fragile daydreams on a canvas.

But he did have the smile of an angel.

★   ★   ★

The ship stayed put till lunchtime the following day. There was a scenic coach drive available, or simply the chance to go ashore again at the small Greek port and spend more time and Euros at the local shops.

We took Aunt Ruby on to dry land for the first time, and had leisurely refreshments in one of those waterside cafes. Everyone bought souvenirs, and we sat sedately writing postcards. Aunt

Dee and I exchanged nudges as we watched Hayden concentrating painfully hard on penning a few lines to his sister Megan.

By the time we trailed back on board, Aunt Ruby was hot, exhausted and irritable. Jamie was coughing. Alicia's face expressed utter boredom.

But the afternoon, with the 'Bella Italia' on the move again, was far brighter — for Cedric was giving another recital in The Studio. 'Restful Music for a Summer Afternoon', Alicia read from the daily news sheet. The two of us took our front row places well before the start.

As ever, the music and its maker gripped and held me. But today I was waiting for it to be over, the final applause, the audience drifting to the exit. I asked Alicia hopefully, 'I believe they're having games and competitions by the big pool, starting right now, so wouldn't you like to — ?'

'No,' she said flatly. 'Sounds like kids' stuff.'

'Then shouldn't you see if Jamie's all right?'

'He's all right. Just his cough, that's all.'

It was then, like a messenger from heaven, a voice hailed us from the doorway: 'Hi, there! — Alicia, I've been looking all over for you!'

Kelly-Ann came straight across to grab the girl's arm.

'I need a table-tennis partner! — if we don't put our names down this minute for the tournament we'll be too late!'

Alicia muttered a sulky imprecation on tables and tennis and over-eager competitors. But she was dragged away. It was really very fortunate.

So fortunate too that today Cedric had time to spare, and the corner of the Deep-Sea Bar was vacant for us. Far, far away was Aunt Ruby's wistful account of a fairytale that faded like a puff of smoke.

We talked about music, his career and mine, where we had played, what we had played. We sat together in our own world. Recalling my time with Grant, so successful and so brief, brought me again to the brink of tears. Cedric held my hand between both of his.

'The sun will come out again for you. If you let it, Lauren. Please believe that.'

I nodded mutely. There was a golden warmth surrounding me already, in his eyes, in his voice, in his gentle touch. I could have stayed there on and on, regardless of time.

It was the advent of a noisy, sun-bronzed group near at hand, laughing and chatting, that shattered the spell. I had been here more than an hour. Reluctantly, I got to my feet.

'I'm not sure about tomorrow, what we'll all be doing — it's my birthday, you see! — '

He said he would look for me anyway. I thought he was going to kiss me. I believed he would have done, but for that raucous group so near to us.

Back in the cabin, Alicia arrived just after I did, hot and shiny-faced but highly pleased with herself. She accused, 'You didn't come to watch. We won! — best of three games against these two French blokes. They were livid.'

'Well done! — I'll watch the next round,' I promised. 'You look like you could use a cool shower!'

She even emerged halfway through it, dripping and towel-draped, to demonstrate her winning shot that had spelt the end for Phillipe and Jean. Indeed, the sun was coming out all round.

There was dinner, with Aunt Ruby somewhat recovered but Jamie still coughing. There was a glitzy show in the big theatre, followed by late light refreshments before bed. It was a warm, still night — and tomorrow we would be in the exotic land of Turkey.

In fact, this was the first night I didn't wake time after time. I even slept late, to be roused by Alicia chanting 'Happy Birthday' and waving a card under my nose.

'I'd buy you something when we go ashore — except I haven't any money.'

'You don't have to buy me anything. The card is lovely!' I sat up to examine its pictured cartoon of a widely grinning cat with the caption, *You're still on your first life, so have a nice day!*

Alicia predicted gloomily, 'Some hopes. Dead boring again.'

'But we're in Turkey, aren't we?'

'I've looked outside, it's only a big town. Sort of industrial.'

'But that'll just be the docks. I bet you it'll be exciting!' I rolled out of bed. 'I'll get ready double quick. We don't want to miss anything.'

She shrugged her stock response, 'Whatever.'

Today's breakfast table was enlivened with more cards. One signed by Hayden (evidently pre-warned) and also in clear rounded letters by Jamie, was a sombre line drawing of St. Paul's Cathedral — as though I wanted to be reminded that a few more days would return me to London.

But Hayden had also achieved something more cheerful. He was explaining to Aunt Ruby, 'As you found yesterday so tiring, Mrs. Pym, I've just been along to the Medical Department, I've arranged to borrow a folding wheelchair for you. All fixed up.'

'What a bright idea!' Aunt Dee beamed. 'Hayden, dear, you're an angel!'

If so, he was a very serious-faced, bespectacled specimen. But it was certainly a helpful idea of his. I felt guilty that he had actually given more thought to my Aunt's problems than I had.

Today's main tour was to the archaeological site of Ephesus, described as 'unmissable'. However, we were missing it — to Alicia's obvious satisfaction. It wasn't a suitable idea for Aunt Ruby, whereas the City Tour would be shorter and easier.

We successfully transferred the old lady from the boat to a waiting motor-coach, where her wheelchair was stowed away, and she and Aunt Dee were given the front seat by our helpful young Turkish guide. A slender, attractive girl with sloe-dark hair and eyes, she introduced herself as 'Emel' — and was consistently addressed by Mrs. Pym as 'Emily'.

To begin with, Izmir appeared a shade disappointing (Alicia nudged me with a triumphant 'Told you!') because of the modern buildings and apartment blocks befitting its status as the third largest city. But relics of an ancient past soon came to light. Emel told us a lot about the agora ('The *what?*' Alicia nudged me again) built by Marcus Aurelius in 178 B.C. When most of us left the coach to visit the Museum's collection of statuary and historic objects, Aunt Ruby remained peacefully snoozing on board with the driver.

But she did leave the vehicle to look around a shopping area, where we had half an hour at leisure. The streets were hot and dusty, and there was plenty of busy, noisy traffic. In the midst of it all, an untimely jangle on my mobile announced a message — from Grant, of all people. In this public place, I just glanced at it.

'Many happy returns, beautiful birthday girl! . . . '

It was enough to carry my thoughts far from the present, so that in a sort of daze I watched Hayden pushing the wheelchair, bending his head to hear what his passenger said. I wanted just to be alone to read Grant's words again, but there was no chance of that. We ended up in a large store where Aunt Ruby directed us firmly to a jewellery counter. I was to choose a gold bangle for my birthday.

It meant trying on several. Alicia watched enviously. Aunt Dee beamed approval.

After that, it was high time to return to the coach. But Aunt Ruby whispered to me, 'Lauren, I must go to the Ladies Room before I get back on that bumpy bus!'

Discreetly I informed the rest of the party. They would go on ahead, and tell Emel we would just be five minutes.

Five minutes! — why had I said five minutes? It had to be a tall order, with the heavy old lady's weight in the chair, in the heat and unfamiliar surroundings. By the time I began trundling her back to the coach we were already well overdue. When I realised I had turned in the wrong direction into a maze of back streets, the sweat was streaming down my face.

'We didn't come this way,' Aunt Ruby started fretting. 'I don't remember any of this! Look, ask that man where the coaches stop!'

The man smiled pleasantly but waved apologetic hands. Two other people did the same.

'Don't worry, it's all right,' I tried to soothe Aunt Ruby. 'I'll text Kelly-Ann, she'll be back on the coach now — isn't it lucky we exchanged numbers yesterday? But — ' It was then that real panic crept into my voice. 'I haven't got my bag! What on earth have I done with my bag? . . . '

Nightmare upon nightmare. No bag, no phone, no money, not to mention no passport or pass card to get back on the ship. Aunt Ruby certainly was clasping her own bulky bag, containing almost everything bar the kitchen sink, but certainly not including a phone. By now she was badly agitated, moaning that she should never have let Dee talk her into leaving her home country.

'Did you leave your bag in that shop? — can you find the way back there? . . . Oh, Lauren, whatever shall we do if the coach goes without us? . . . oh, do you know what time the boat sails? . . . '

'They won't go without us,' I kept on saying, not very convincingly because with every passing minute my own panic was beginning to match hers. 'Auntie, I'm so very sorry about all this. I'll find someone in a minute who speaks English. There's got to be someone around here who speaks English! — '

'Will I do?' a quiet voice said behind me.

I spun round, almost overcome by the vastness of my relief. Hayden looked nearly as hot and bothered as we were, but he stooped to reassure the distressed old lady very kindly. She was visibly shaking, and amazingly he held her for a moment in a warm, consoling hug.

'Come on, Aunt Ruby. You're safe now. No harm done.'

'Hayden, I — I thought — ' she quavered. 'We were lost and — I thought we'd be left behind . . . and — and I'm so helpless, I can't . . . '

'I know. But it's all right now. And I wouldn't have allowed the coach to move till you were back on it.'

He turned to me then, and I realised I was shaking as well, with the reaction to this very bad dream. And surely I was still dreaming? — for those comforting arms surrounded me too.

I just clung to him. At that moment, I would have clung to anyone.

He said quietly, 'Shall we get started? I know the way back to the coach — I think!'

4

There was general relief when we arrived at the waiting coach. Aunt Dee, most of all, was almost speechless. A few people volunteered bright suggestions — so easy, after the event — like, 'You could have got a taxi back to the boat and let the security people sort it all out!' — or, 'Why didn't you just draw a picture of a coach?' They didn't explain how to produce pen and paper from thin air.

From our young Turkish guide came no recriminations, just sympathy and cold reviving drinks. Readily I took all the blame for the mishap: 'I got distracted — but I was a complete idiot to turn in the wrong direction!' It was touching that Aunt Ruby spoke up for me, insisting the mistake was easily made in a strange place — 'And no-one could have been kinder to a tiresome old woman!'

No-one but the remote and glacial Hayden Jardine, I thought. He waved aside any outpourings of gratitude. He had guessed I would be somewhere near that big shop, trying to find my missing bag — which wasn't missing at all, but in Alicia's keeping! Of course, she had held it for me while I tried on the gold bangles.

'Here.' She planted it in my lap. 'You went off in a rush, I didn't get a chance to give it back.'

I received it with still more relief. As well, with a niggling question in my mind: should I count my money and possessions, or not even think it? . . .

Back on the ship for a late lunch, my head was still whirling. I hadn't yet answered Grant's message. Was he sitting waiting for it? Was Elaine there waiting with him? I could hardly swallow any food, or attend to trivial chat around the table.

Eventually I managed to escape to a corner of the big lounge with my phone. At that exact moment, a call came through from my cousin Tina.

'Hello there! Happy birthday! Are you having a good day?'

'Wonderful,' I lied in my teeth.

'That's good. I couldn't send your pressie, but it's here waiting. And I've lots of news! That puzzle you set me, I think I've done an excellent job for you, Miss Roache. The school is St. Luke's, your Mr. Jardine was Head of the Maths Department. There was a major scandal, more like an earthquake — it was in the local newspaper at the time. I made more enquiries as well.'

I whispered, 'What sort of a scandal?'

'You have to understand, this is quite a prestigious school, highly respected. One of the institutions is the annual Chalfont Bursary, founded by Sir Dennis Chalfont, an ex-pupil. Worth quite a lot of money for future education. Well, this time — shock horror! — it seems one of the exam papers was leaked, and a pupil notori-ous for disruptive behaviour and an aversion to working, submitted a near-perfect entry. Are you with me?'

I didn't want to be with her. But I asked, 'Maths, of course?'

'Of course. So heavy suspicion fell on friend Hayden for wickedly tipping the wink to his daughter. The newspaper mentioned a public scene at the School's auspicious Prize Day — insults flying like autumn leaves. I gather Hayden told the Headmaster what to do with his exam results, himself, and his Board of Governors.'

'Hayden did?' I muttered. There were indeed unsuspected facets to the man.

'Indeed. Afterwards, he and his daughter left the place suddenly and simultaneously. Doesn't sound too healthy, does it?'

'It sounds awful. But I just can't believe Hayden would do something dishonest! . . . ' I was too aghast to ask all the questions flooding my mind. 'Is — is that all?'

'All about the school, but there's more news. I saw Grant last night. He sends you his love and hopes you're having a fabulous time. He was very cheerful! — quite sprightly, pleased to see me, ready to chat. And he told me — the date is fixed for his wedding to Elaine. About six weeks time, all the arrangements being made, and we'll both be invited.'

I had no voice, no breath, almost no feeling. After a moment Tina's voice came again across the miles.

'Laurie, did you hear me? Are you okay?'

'I'm okay.' It sounded like a stranger's voice answering her. 'That's nice for them.'

'Yes. He said he must practise with his new buggy so he can trundle down the aisle without running the vicar over. — Well, so where have you folks been today? . . . '

I told her where we went, not mentioning the panic of getting lost — which was partly, indeed, due to receiving Grant's birthday greeting. I told her the next two days we would be in Istanbul. I thanked her for finding out so much information.

After that stressful conversation, the afternoon seemed to last for ever. Numbly I watched Alicia and Kelly-Ann sail through to the next round of the table-tennis. I sat in the sun with a book I never read.

'You poor love,' Aunt Dee sympathised, 'that mix-up this morning has really upset you, hasn't it? Never mind, we've a lovely surprise for you this evening!'

I wanted no lovely surprises, just a certain hour to come. When it did, I slipped down to a lower deck, to that secluded corner in the Deep Sea Bar — and there a man was sitting already at what had become 'our' table.

'Hello, a very happy birthday!' He nodded across to the serving counter, and in a moment two bubbling glasses arrived. 'Yes, champagne! — what else could I order today?'

'That's nice,' I muttered. In a few weeks, I would be expected to celebrate with more champagne, to toast Grant and Elaine's future together.

'There's something else I've planned,' Cedric was saying softly. 'The Studio is all empty, the piano is waiting for us. You could play for me today? I so much want to hear you play . . . '

'Don't ask, I can't! I told you before!' The words were like a cry of pain.

'Because of your friend and the accident. But you said he is better?'

'He is. So much that he's getting married in a few weeks,' I blurted out. 'Oh, I'm being very bitter and selfish to mind, it's wonderful for him! But — '

'For you, not wonderful. He was more than a friend, so it hurts.'

I looked into his eyes, that were filled now with concern. 'It does hurt. I think — I loved him a lot, I didn't know how much. How do you just stop loving someone?'

'I never found that out. There was a girl I knew — Maria was a nurse at the hospital when I was ill. Maria.' He repeated the name softly. 'The only thing is just to move on. As best that

107

you can, move on. I'm not telling you it's easy.'

I nodded, and with quick sympathy I reached for his hand. It closed on mine. Neither of us finished the birthday champagne. We sat there in our corner, almost in silence, our hands and our thoughts joined.

It was enough. The first sharpness of my pain was a little soothed. When I stood up at last to leave, he kissed me, just a touch on my cheek. He said softly, 'For your birthday.'

The shadowed world wasn't quite devoid of sunlight. This 'enchanted voyage' wasn't quite bereft of wonder.

Coming from that dreamlike interlude back to reality, I discovered tonight was scheduled as 'The Captain's Gala Dinner'. Alicia pointed it out gloomily in the cabin. I made a huge effort at cheery interest.

'So we wheel out the posh frocks! How does this grab you, Alicia?'

I had packed just one of the creations I wore on stage with Grant, the one he specially liked: gracefully long, halter-necked, it had a sequined shimmer down the slender skirt. Its pale aqua did show off the golden tan I was acquiring. The girl's eyes opened wider as I pirouetted for approval.

'Wow!' was her verdict.

Exactly Grant's reaction, with that bright smile of his that so haunted me. I wondered, would Cedric think the same?

On our dinner table, the first part of Aunt Dee's 'surprise' was at once obvious: a few packages wrapped in fancy paper and ribbon. Her gift was a silver photo-frame. From Hayden came a book describing the history and geography of the regions we were visiting (I wondered, should I ink in my name and class number on the fly-leaf?) Jamie's present was a 'Bella Italia' pencil: Alicia's (but how did she pay for it?) a floaty scarf.

I donned the scarf at once, to go with Aunt Ruby's gold bangle. I made an embarrassed speech of general thanks.

But that was only the start of my embarrassment — for during the meal a group of broadly smiling waiters encircled our table to sing me a romantic serenade. There was applause from the surrounding tables. From a distance I saw Kelly-Ann and Joey convulsed with laughter.

Nor had Aunt Dee finished yet.

'Now then, dear, I thought we'd give the Show a miss today — you don't mind? — '

I minded, if it meant missing Cedric too. But what could I say?

'There's something I've earmarked for you!' She quoted from today's timetable: ''*For our UK guests, an Olde-Tyme Supper Dance, come and dance the evening away in the old fashioned way! . . . *''

There was no escape. Not even for Alicia, whose disgust seemed beyond words — until we reached The Studio to find the seating ranged around the walls and a modest ensemble of musicians sorting themselves and their instruments out on the stage. There was a guitar, a drums-and-percussion set, and the piano. The pianist was Cedric.

Alicia marched straight up to him, and I saw him showing her his music sheets. She actually looked interested. He glanced across at me, standing here like a spare part in my gorgeous gown, and nodded and smiled. With people all around, far away were our private, secret moments.

I knew about Olde Tyme dances, because Aunt Dee had taught me various steps when I was a child, and we even entered a local contest together and gained a 'commended'. It was a sweet thought of hers that I would like this on my birthday, and I tried not to disappoint her. We took the floor together in quite a stylish fashion. It was like riding a bike, she said, you didn't forget.

But I wasn't able to monopolise her, because an elderly military-looking gentleman, with steel-blue eyes and a clipped white moustache, kept approaching to ask her for a dance. I exchanged a grin with Aunt Ruby, who was sitting in a corner eyeing the passing dancers critically up and down and tapping her stick to the music. Jamie, beside her, was struggling to keep awake. Alicia had parked herself near Cedric to watch him play.

Which left only one option. 'No wallflowers allowed,' Aunt Dee said briskly. 'Come on, Lauren — Hayden — on your feet!'

Hayden's dismayed protest had no effect at all.

'This is a waltz, dear. *Everyone* can waltz.'

She glided off gracefully in the arms of her military gentleman — and I glided off, more or less, with Mr. H. Jardine, late Head of Maths. I couldn't quite believe it. Impossibly, this was the second time today he had held me in his arms.

He apologised, 'Sorry about the two left feet.' He was actually blushing in embarrassment, which somehow made him look less remote. His highly correct dark suit contrasted with his flushed face and the almost flaxen fairness of his hair.

Trying to ignore trampled-on toes, I encouraged him, 'We're doing fine, serious opposition to Astaire and Rogers. Listen, I must thank you again for the rescue this morning. I've never been more pleased to see anyone in my life!'

'I'm sure there's a procedure for lost passengers. You wouldn't have been abandoned to your fate.'

'Well, it felt like we were! On my own I'd have muddled through, but — '

'I know, it was very difficult with the old lady. I feel partly to blame, I should have hung around for you. Only I wanted to get Jamie back to the coach.'

I said, 'Of course,' just stifling an 'ouch!'

'At least Aunt Ruby seems none the worse.' (More and more he was dropping the formal 'Mrs. Pym'.) 'And I noticed she ate quite a good dinner.

Usually she treats every course as a heart attack on a plate.'

I giggled at that. For once, he was quite chatty and approachable. Sincerely I asked, 'I hope you're enjoying this cruise! — are you?'

'It was very kind of your Aunt to include us.'

'Certainly, but that's not what I asked! Are you enjoying it?'

'I'm trying. I do have rather a lot on my mind at present.'

This was an opportunity unlikely to be repeated. Without pausing to consider, I plunged.

'I know you have. Forgive me, but — I've found out about St. Luke's, what you were supposed to have done. I'd like to say, I don't for a moment believe you were purposely dishonest! But — if you were under a huge pressure of work, you might have been a little careless? — it's so easy to forget to lock things up if you're tired and stressed! And if Alicia was stressed too, and temptation was just sitting there beckoning, perhaps — ?'

My voice petered out, and so did our efforts to circle the dance floor. We had landed in an empty corner, and his arms no longer held me. Visibly he had reverted to his chilly usual self.

'That's an interesting theory. Wholly incorrect. I didn't gain a position of responsibility by crumbling under pressure.' His pale eyes were stern and stony behind their strong, gold-framed lenses. 'I wondered why Alicia was so keen to enter the exam, I agreed against my better judgment — I admit to that. I didn't realise at the time she was cold-bloodedly scheming to ruin my career. She obviously had a duplicate key made to my study at home, and photocopied my master sheets for the Bursary Exam.'

The cold, quiet voice chilled me through. I exclaimed, shakily with shock, 'Hayden! Please! We're talking about a twelve year old child!'

'A child with a lot of intelligence and a lot of hate.'

'For pity's sake, man!' I burst out, vaguely aware of startled heads turning our way. 'All right, she can be a real pain! — but *how* does that make her a — a dyed-in-the-wool criminal? — '

'It's not rocket science to understand how and why. She can't forgive me for marrying her mother. I broke up their cosy life together — and so in the end caused poor Nancy's death. That's not just a theory, that's fact — if it's any of your business!'

I stood there just gazing at him. It was a relief that the music ended and people were drifting back to their seats. Aunt Dee was signalling rather anxiously across to ask if we wanted a drink. Somehow I hoisted a smile on to my face as I turned my back on Hayden and started off towards her.

Indeed, I had discovered deep, dark waters. Deeper and darker than the dim tide sliding past the 'Bella Italia' in the still, balmy night.

★   ★   ★

In the cabin, as we went to bed, Alicia commented, 'He's rubbish, isn't he? Have you got any toes left?'

'A few. Not every man is a Terpsichorean expert, you know.'

'A what? Can I borrow your after-sun lotion?'

I looked across at her as she brushed her long hair. Clad in a brief nightshirt with some cartoon animal cavorting on the front, for once she looked far less than twelve years old. In fact, tomorrow she would be thirteen, as our birthdays fell on consecutive days: one of those coincidences after all not so very strange.

It was on the tip of my tongue to repeat to her Hayden's rather appalling words, but I didn't do that. It was essential not to plunge in headfirst as I mostly did, but to choose exactly the right moment. Most of all, I mustn't make matters worse.

She was saying, 'If I get any of those singing waiters tomorrow, I shall jump overboard, I promise you!'

I undertook to mention it to Aunt Dee, lest she had any schemes afoot. Alicia watched for a few minutes more the progress of the ship on the TV screen, the little pulsating dot creeping its way across the map.

When we settled down for the night, I kept thinking about Grant's 'beautiful birthday girl' message, and the brief, stilted reply I eventually sent back. I thought of Cedric's hand holding mine, and his sad advice about 'moving on'. I thought of Hayden, a difficult, troubled, embittered man, so hard to reach.

The morning brought us another blaze of sunshine, and brought too the strikingly picturesque shoreline of Istanbul, mosques pointing their slender minarets skywards, huddled buildings, a sweep of blue water crisscrossed by busy boats.

'*This colourful, fascinating city, straddling Asia and Europe, offers many varied delights,*' I read impressively from our daily bulletin. 'Come on, Alicia, no lazing in bed just because you're a teenager!'

My gift for her was waiting: a selection of perfume and shampoo and other interesting bottles and jars, and a tee-shirt with an embroidered TURKIYE across the front. I had expected her to shrug an indifferent 'Thanks a bunch' in her usual careless way. Instead, she gazed at the present for a long silent moment, and I saw her lip quiver.

'I hope you're pleased,' I said softly. 'I didn't know what to get — '

'It's nice. It's all nice!'

Just briefly, without fuss, I put my arm round her. Was it possible she could be the malicious young schemer Hayden believed? Whatever her faults, maybe many and varied, wouldn't a little love and understanding surely help her more than any amount of disgrace and punishment?

Our breakfast table was devoid of vocalising waiters, but it did present an array of cards and gifts. Hayden's card (about as sombre as the one he gave to me) contained some money: not a lot of money. She glanced across the table with a gruff mumble of thanks.

He didn't improve the moment by commenting, 'Make sure you buy something sensible.'

'Now, Hayden, dear!' Aunt Dee admonished. 'When you're just thirteen you're entitled to buy something not at all sensible. Alicia, there'll be lots of nice things to choose in Istanbul!'

The day's programme was to include a drive around the City, a visit to some of the mosques and the Topkapi Palace. It wasn't the longest tour on offer, in deference to Aunt Ruby. When we assembled in the theatre to receive our numbered stickers and instructions, it was nice to find we were again in the charge of yesterday's sympathetic guide.

'Good morning, Emily,' Aunt Ruby hailed her. 'I'm afraid you're landed with us again!'

Whatever her private thoughts, the girl answered with her bright smile, 'It's a pleasure to have you, Mrs. Pym, I'm sure no big troubles today!'

On the coach we were once more

rearranged, because Aunt Dee insisted, 'I'm sitting with the birthday girl!' I found myself partnering Jamie. So far, I hadn't got to know the little boy very well, and it seemed a good chance to remedy that.

His blue eyes were shyly downcast, his fair face had coloured up. But surprisingly he observed, 'Che bella giorna!'

'A beautiful day? — yes, it is! Who taught you that, Jamie?'

'Giuseppe did. He teaches my Dad and me new words every day.'

Typical, I thought. Doubtless arranged by Mr. Stay-in-after-class Jardine, unable to miss a chance of turning any holidays into lesson-times. But the idea faded as the minutes went by. I watched Jamie constantly craning his neck to make sure Hayden was sitting safely two rows ahead with Aunt Ruby. I was remembering that sensational story of the garage robbery. Jamie clearly adored his father, had been shattered by that terrifying incident, and was uneasy at being parted from him even briefly — as witness, of course, his extreme reaction on our very first day together when Hayden was singled out for a security search.

I asked gently, 'Would you like to change places?'

'No. It's all right. It's just — ' He wriggled awkwardly. 'Did you know about how he got hurt? We were coming back from taking Ally to stay over at Auntie Megan's, and we had to get some petrol, and — '

'I know, darling. Don't think about it.'

'We had to go in an ambulance. It had all its hooters hooting . . . ' When he frowned, there was Hayden in his face. 'I thought they'd killed him dead. All his face was bandaged up . . . and Ally and me had to stay with Aunt Megan . . . she's got a big garden, she lets me feed her rabbit, but . . . '

'I know what happened, Jamie,' I whispered again as his voice broke. 'Please, don't think about it.'

'Well, but — ' He wriggled still more.

'Auntie Megan told us we've got to look after him 'cos he can't see properly any more. Ally says it's a silly fuss, but — but I do try — '

'I'm sure you do.' I put a tentative arm round him, and it was pleasing that he nestled into it. 'Don't worry, your Dad's a very strong person. He'll be fine! Look at him now, pointing things out to Aunt Ruby. Let's just enjoy this exciting place, shall we?'

I did my best to interest him in the more or less chaotic Istanbul streets, the colourful shops, the tramcars, the careering yellow taxis that seemed to zigzag a charmed path through the congestion. Presently we toured around on foot, with Aunt Ruby's wheelchair duly unfolded. We admired the impressive spectacle of The Blue Mosque — the Mosque of Sultan Ahmet I, Emel told us — with its six lofty minarets, its great dome and beautiful tiles. We saw the equally picturesque Mosque of Hagia Sophia nearby. We also viewed the site of the historic Hippodrome in the heart of the Old Town.

As for the famous Topkapi Palace, the displays in the Museum — diamonds and glassware, kaftans and helmets, bejewelled daggers — were all quite breathtaking. Even Alicia was enthralled by the jewels. But it was very warm, and it was tiring: I noticed Hayden and Jamie sitting by the entrance waiting for us — and laughed to hear Jamie trying to read aloud the Turkish words on his entrance pass. Almost I asked severely, 'So where's your Turkish dictionary, Mr. Jardine, don't tell me you left it behind? . . . '

Emel found time to read out slowly all the print on the ticket in Turkish and English, and complimented a shyly delighted Jamie on his interest. She was keeping an exceptionally close eye on our party today. I didn't at all blame her.

We had a brief stop at the Topkapi's terrace café, looking across a vista of close-packed land and blue water while we sipped ice-cold fruit juice. It seemed a shame to leave it all behind and head back to the coach.

On board the ship all too soon for lunch, there was still plenty of afternoon left for table-tennis, a session in the pool (I could still get into my brief black swimsuit) and a General Knowledge Quiz in the library — which Hayden naturally won hands down. I just hoped Alicia was enjoying her day. It was hard to tell.

My thoughts had long been turning to this evening's Show, and before it a stolen few minutes with Cedric. Only a few minutes, as another musician was unwell and he needed to 'fill in'. Today, as well, I couldn't ditch Alicia — an unkind thought. He gave her a tiny package containing two diamante hair-grips. She actually beamed her delight.

What he gave me was a moment of nearness, the touch of his hand on my arm. More precious than all the chilly glitter of those Topkapi jewels.

We all retired late that night, after lingering on deck in the warm dusk beneath festoons of coloured lights. Remote from the City's noise and bustle, we looked out on the fairytale vista of Istanbul, the illuminated domes and fingers of the mosques against the dark sky. Even Aunt Ruby seemed mesmerised by the scene. I heard her telling her sister, 'You know, Dee, poor dear Mario could paint a wonderful picture of all this . . . '

'With you standing in the foreground in your long white dress,' Aunt Dee agreed.

'Hmph! These days I'd look like a sack of wet washing.'

'My dear, beauty is in the eye of the beholder. But I really think it's time for bed, we're out again early tomorrow . . . '

Tomorrow would bring a 'carpet demonstration', whatever that meant, and the Grand Bazaar. And then goodbye to Turkey, and just one more port of call — just one! — before returning to Venice for a plane home: back to my disordered life without music, a future I hadn't in any way sorted out. Unless, maybe, the smile in a man's eyes was already clearing a way for me?

From sheer weariness I slept as soon as my head was on the pillow. But it seemed only moments later that I woke suddenly, aware of nearby disturbing noises. Alicia was sobbing out broken words: 'I didn't . . . I *didn't*! . . . *why* can't you believe me? . . . '

Though I tried to wake her gently, her eyes opened wide in fright. She was still sobbing almost hysterically.

'It's all right, you were just dreaming. Just a bad dream, Ally.'

She was shaking, her hair wild, her face hot and tear-stained. She drew back quickly from my attempt at a comforting hug.

'If there's something worrying you,' I said softly, 'would it help to talk about it, just the two of us? Or talk to Aunt Dee, she's helped me with problems many times? — '

She shook her head. I tried again, 'Or

how about your Auntie Megan?'

'No!' she refused curtly.

I took a deep breath. This time, in my usual fashion, I plunged straight in.

'Were you dreaming about that Bursary Exam? Did you really cheat to get your — your new Dad into trouble? Is that what's bothering you?'

She was almost herself again by now, coolly staring at me. She answered insolently, 'Wouldn't you like to know?'

'Yes, I would! Because — he isn't exactly a well man, is he? Your Aunt Megan told me — and Jamie's really worried about him — '

'Oh, she fusses over nothing! And Jamie is just his Daddy's little diddums.'

'I don't believe it's a fuss over nothing,' I said quietly. 'Your Dad needs help and support from you. And so does Jamie. They need it right now.'

She stared at me a moment more, and then shrugged her shoulders.

'I'm tired, I want to sleep. Do you mind?'

I stood up with a sigh. The moment

had come and gone, and time was running out. For all of us, it was. When we stepped ashore for the final time, it seemed the Jardines still would be a broken family. I must still face moving on from Grant . . .

Yet again the thought came to me, if I might move on with Cedric Raphael — wouldn't at least one sunburst come from so many shadows?

* * *

'Shopping!' Kelly-Ann gloated at a hasty early breakfast. 'Lots and lots of shopping!'

At their table near ours, her sober-faced husband looked alarmed. Joey was plastering jam an inch thick on his bread. I agreed, 'Shop till we drop! — can't be bad!'

Alicia seemed very subdued and heavy-eyed this morning, even though the Grand Bazaar was a variation on venerable buildings. I wondered if she had slept as little as I had.

It was another occasion for Aunt Ruby to greet our guide, 'Good morning, it's us again, Emily!' Maybe the girl had already applied for 'time-and-a-half' for taking care of our party, but she was as polite as ever. Once on the coach, she informed us all that the first stop would be an exhibition of the country's highly prized carpets: 'And a chance to taste our very much delicious apple tea, ladies and gentlemen, I'm sure you'll enjoy it.'

We were dropped near some sort of large store or warehouse, and led to a spacious apartment with chairs around the walls, where a couple of well-muscled young men carried in a series of large rolls of carpet and unrolled them expertly in our midst. The hues and designs were truly beautiful. Unfortunately, so many flapping carpets started Jamie coughing, and Hayden took him outside. They missed the trays of teacups that were brought in: the drink was pleasant enough — though I spotted Alicia, freed from

Hayden's watchful gaze, clutching her throat and rolling her eyes in a crude representation of nausea. Joey gleefully followed her lead.

Afterwards came the Grand Bazaar. Indeed, I wasn't quite prepared for the vast area full of bustle and chatter, innumerable stalls and shops displaying all kinds of clothing, jewellery, bric-a-brac and trinkets. Emel advised us, 'Don't stop to tie up your shoe or you'll be sold all of everything in sight!'

It was even more amazing to see Aunt Ruby enter energetically into the spirit of the place, proving herself an indomitable 'haggler' with the vendors. She collected a number of carrier-bags — presents, she said, even one for a neighour, 'that Mrs. Kirby opposite'.

She wasn't the only one concerned with presents.

'Lauren, could you spare a moment?' Hayden muttered to me. We had scarcely spoken since last night's heated words on the dance floor. 'I need to find a thank-you gift for Aunt Dee. If you can help at all — '

'Oh! Yes, I'll try,' I agreed readily. 'I was thinking the same thing. We just passed a place with some gorgeous cushions — all beads and fringes, she'd love them.'

We lagged behind the others to investigate the sumptuous cushions, and ended up sharing the cost of four, plus a settee-throw and table-cover. It entailed carting along a couple of huge bags. They drew inquisitive glances when we caught up with the others.

'What are they?' Alicia wanted to know. She had spent her birthday money on a pretty silver chain, and it seemed to have brightened her mood. I put a finger to my lips and nodded towards Aunt Dee, and she nodded back conspiratorially.

Though we had really seen only part of the Bazaar, it was nearing the time to meet up with the coach. It was very hot now, the sun blazing down on busy streets. A nearby café with pavement tables and sunshades looked like a welcome oasis. There was just time for a cooling drink.

'My treat, everybody!' Aunt Dee insisted as we sat down companionably around a table. But the amiable atmosphere was too good to last. When Alicia tipped back her chair and put her feet on another, Hayden's sharp public rebuke started a storm.

'You're always picking on me! Jamie's spilt some of his drink — and Lauren's slurping hers — but oh no, it has to be me! — '

The altercation didn't last long. She jumped to her feet, sending one of the chairs clattering over, and made off rapidly along the pavement. We were all taken by surprise. In just a moment she had vanished among the crowds and traffic.

It was equally surprising to hear Hayden swear softly but quite forcefully as he jumped up to pursue her. So perhaps he was human after all? But in his hurry, he tripped on one of those giant carrier-bags parked by his chair.

Thrown right off balance he staggered and clutched vainly at a table, and staggered again, until he fell heavily flat on his face.

Aunt Dee exclaimed, 'My dear boy! . . . ' Jamie burst into tears. It was a huge relief that Hayden was attempting to get up. Two of the friendly café staff rushed over to help him into a chair.

'You okay, sir? . . . you want come inside, you need doctor? . . . '

'Thanks, I'm all right,' Hayden was trying to say.

He didn't look all right. And it was just at that moment that I saw Alicia strolling quite casually back. She had probably just been hiding in a doorway.

Gone were all thoughts of using careful tact and diplomacy to help along a difficult relationship. I fairly screamed at her, 'Now do you see the trouble your silly, stupid, pig-headed behaviour causes? I hope you're ashamed of yourself! I'm sorry I've wasted so much time on you! — '

She stared at me, deeply shocked, and as well deeply hurt. At this moment, I didn't care what she felt.

I realised that someone else had got up to help, from another table where a few of our fellow-travellers were sitting — actually it was Major Battersby, Aunt Dee's 'military gent'. He was salvaging something from the roadway, where it had been flung under passing wheels. He held it out to me.

'The young man's glasses. What's left of them. Too bad, I hope he brought a spare pair away with him.'

'So do I,' I said quietly. 'So do I.'

5

It was fortunate that the coach was just a few minutes away. When at last we set out for it, I thrust the heaviest of the bags at Alicia with the terse instruction, 'Carry it!' Aunt Ruby had the other on her lap in her wheelchair, and Major Battersby helpfully shunted her along. Aunt Dee was comforting a still pale and shaky Jamie.

Which left me free to reach for Hayden's hand in protective fashion.

'Hang on to me,' I invited. 'We can't have any more collapses in the gutter, it'll get our party a bad name!'

I fully expected to be rebuffed. Instead, he gripped my hand tightly. He even murmured, 'Thanks.'

'It must have shaken you up. She can be a little monster! But she couldn't have guessed — '

'Of course not. She just wanted to

aggravate me — as usual.'

We were overtaken then by our guide and a few more of the coach passengers. Emel gazed at our bedraggled group almost in disbelief as the story was poured out to her by various witnesses.

'We have first aid equipments on the coach, Mr. Jardine,' she told him anxiously. 'And I can phone ahead to the ship — '

'Please,' he interrupted her shortly, 'don't bother, I'm fine. I'm fine!'

He seemed indeed less hurt than quite simply furious: furious with Alicia, with himself for falling — most of all for the loss of that very important pair of spectacles. The hard grip of his hand on mine made me wonder, exactly how important?

I ventured to ask if he had spare glasses, and was answered briefly, 'Of course, but they're an old prescription — so like a raving idiot I left them at home.' I didn't comment on that.

However, by the time we were all

settled again on the coach, he and I still together, some of his anger seemed to have boiled away. He looked worried and weary, frowning painfully in the light. Unusually, he slumped back in his seat.

I said quite gently, 'Perhaps you should know — that affair at the petrol station, I know what happened. I think you were very brave to try to intervene.'

'I don't know about brave. It was a damn-fool thing to do, but I was afraid for Jamie — and the whole thing made me *angry*. I didn't see why they should get away with it. Anyway, they did.'

'I know. And it left you with these serious eye problems. It's not a bit fair.'

'Life seldom is fair.' He added, but no longer irritably, 'You're quite a Sherlock Holmes on the quiet, aren't you?'

'Sorry! I must seem like a real busybody. But you see, I needed to find out everything surrounding Alicia. She's so young — and so unhappy. I've been trying to help her.'

'I know you have. And I do appreciate it.'

'Oh,' I muttered, more and more surprised. The Istanbul streets slipping past the windows could have been in Iceland or Australia for all I saw of them. For the first time that chilly front he presented to the world had completely melted. The sigh he gave was tired, despondent, almost despairing.

'Poor Alicia. She hadn't got over losing her father when I butted in and married Nancy. She was wildly jealous. All over again when Jamie was born. He had delicate health from day one, he took all the limelight. I daresay things were handled wrongly . . .'

I whispered, 'I'm sure you did your best.'

'Then it wasn't good enough, was it? I wanted us to be a family, that's all I ever wanted. But I doubt it'll ever happen now. I've been thinking seriously of sending Alicia off to live at my sister's for a year or two, Megan did offer to take her.'

'But wouldn't that be admitting defeat?' I asked earnestly. 'And think, Denny — ' (The pet name must be on my lips through recalling my conversation with Megan?) 'Just think, you'll need some help and support if your eyesight keeps getting worse. Alicia should be with you to give it! She should!'

'Hardly likely, is it?' He smiled wryly. 'Repentant child rushes to aid and comfort hated but stricken step-father? No, I think not. Not when her chief satisfaction seems to be having ruined my teaching career.'

There seemed no answer to that. We sat for a moment in heavy silence until he spoke again, very quietly.

'I believe I was a good teacher, Lauren. I put my heart and soul into it. It's the one thing I've been really proud of.'

'You can be again. I'm sure you can!'

'And pigs can fly. But — thanks for the encouragement.'

'I mean it. And I've been wanting to

say to you — Alicia is really very musical, so is it quite fair to keep the piano locked up at home?'

'I don't know. It seemed a good idea at the time, a good way to punish her for — all sorts of things. It was Nancy's piano. They used to play it together.'

'And after you lost Nancy, it hurt you too much to hear it?' I suggested softly.

'Maybe. So you're not just a Sherlock Holmes, you're a Dr. Freud as well?'

'I hope I'm — a friend. You all seem as though you need one.'

His hand just lightly squeezed mine. There was no time for more, for already the coach was pulling up, with the white bulk of the ship looming nearby. Strangely, I wanted the ride to be longer.

For the short walk to the gangway, Aunt Dee took Hayden's arm in her ever-kindly way, telling him he looked quite groggy and must lie down this afternoon for a rest. I overheard Aunt Ruby telling Emel, who was holding Jamie's hand, 'I'm sure you're glad to be rid of *us*, Emily dear!'

Jamie whispered to the girl shyly, 'Grazie mille!' — the wrong language, but it didn't matter. I resolved to commend her to the management, surely the least we could do!

Lunch wasn't a very enjoyable meal, with Hayden and Jamie scarcely eating a morsel, and Aunt Ruby forecasting darkly that the lasagne had enough garlic in it to curdle anyone's insides despite a double dose of Dr. Wright's. Afterwards came the usual mix of activities for people not inclined to roast their tans a shade darker on the sun deck. For a wonder, Hayden did agree to rest, leaving an anxious Jamie in our collective care. Alicia sat by herself in the big lounge, trying to avoid contact with anyone.

But when the time approached for Cedric's 'Music to Remember' in The Studio she awoke suddenly to life. I already had Jamie in tow while the Aunts rested. It meant two companions as I sat in the front row, drinking in the music note by note.

Halfway through, Jamie fell asleep, nestled against me. After the closing encore, as the audience dispersed, Cedric came and sat beside me. He allowed Alicia her usual 'Five minutes, *pianissimo*!' at the piano, and she launched into some halting, mournful Chopin.

I muttered rather wearily, 'I'm not sure she deserves it today.'

'Trouble?'

'Big trouble! I'm afraid her family is always trouble.'

I didn't want to think now of the luckless Jardines. These present moments were so precious, and so very brief.

Cedric talked about the Lullaby he had just played — 'It worked too well,' he said, 'to send my audience to sleep.' But then Jamie grunted and stretched. His pale-blue eyes — Hayden's eyes — looked all around in alarm.

'It's all right, sweetheart.' I gave him a reassuring squeeze. 'Your Daddy's just having a little rest. Let's go and find him now!'

So Alicia's meagre five minutes were mine too. Cedric whispered to me, 'I'm in the Show tonight. You'll be there, please?'

Could he doubt it for even a moment?

* * *

We waved goodbye to Turkey that same evening. Tomorrow would be a full day at sea: no shore excursions, so surely no chance for any more major misfortunes — unless one of our party fell overboard? I didn't entirely rule that out!

Our dinner table was enlivened by two minor eruptions. The first happened when Jamie (I was discovering now and then quite another side to shy, timid Jamie) gravely greeted our waiter Eugenio, 'Buona sera, come sta?' Alicia muttered, 'Show-off!' and Jamie flared back at her, 'Giuseppi taught me, he's taught me lots, so there!'

Hayden told them both to mind their

manners or leave the table.

After that, I made the mistake of admiring Aunt Ruby's amber necklace, and she snorted, 'It doesn't match this dress, I'd have worn my gold locket — if I could find it!'

Alicia sipped her orange juice with an air of aggrieved innocence. Her face didn't change at all, no guilty flush, no averted gaze.

Aunt Dee suggested mildly, 'Ruby, maybe you just didn't bring it with you?' Her sister crushed that idea, 'I'm not quite senile yet, I saw it here the first day we came!'

A fortunate diversion was the spectacular 'Baked Alaska Ceremony', with a marching line of white-garbed, tall-hatted chefs carrying their flaming platters of the exotic dessert through the darkened restaurant.

For me, the meal was just a time-passing prelude to the evening Show, for Cedric's interval recital. I caught Aunt Ruby's shrewd eyes upon me as I listened and watched with my ears and my eyes and my heart.

But this was far away from that sad, romantic tale she had told me, the beautiful young girl, the charming footloose artist! That was her life, not mine. Her life, her fond, nostalgic memory cherished over so many years . . .

'Mind you get a good night's sleep, Ally!' Kelly-Ann called out to Alicia as I opened our cabin door. 'Table tennis finals tomorrow — and we're going to win!' She added to me quietly, 'Lauren, is your — er — friend all right? I thought he didn't look well tonight.'

'Hayden? — oh, he tripped over and smashed his glasses.'

'Oh!' She dismissed that lightly, as anyone might. 'Tough! He needs to take more water with it! Night-night, see you tomorrow, folks.'

She seemed to live such a sunny, uncomplicated life. I wondered how she managed it.

I hadn't really spoken to Alicia since my fierce outburst at the café, and with the good intention of not letting the sun go down on my wrath I made an effort to clear the air while we prepared for bed.

'Sorry I yelled at you like I did. Of course, you didn't know there'd be an accident.'

She shrugged her shoulders. 'It's all right.'

'But it's not really, is it?' I insisted. 'You could try helping your Dad instead of bothering him. Ally, is he still having treatment for his eyes?'

'He's got an appointment when we get back. He's had lots.'

'Well, then!' I said gently.

'He doesn't want any help from me. He doesn't want me around at all.'

'I'm quite sure that's not true. Did he ever tell you that?'

'I *know*!' she said doggedly.

She plumped down on to her bed and pulled the cover over her head with a terse ''Night!'

Well, I had tried. Yet again, I had. While there was still a little time left, I would go on trying.

The new morning brought another beautiful day, a sparkling blue sea, a long white trail in the huge vessel's wake. But the hours dragged a little. It seemed to me as though things were already winding down.

There was the table-tennis, of course, which meant cheering on Kelly-Ann and Alicia; in the end they were actually runners-up. There was some amusement about Aunt Dee's 'military gent' — Major Rupert Battersby, we now knew him to be — cornering her for coffee and cards, and inviting her to visit his Cotswolds village next month for its annual Flower Festival. But for me the day's highlight was a 'Musical Quiz', which Cedric conducted in The Studio with piano illustrations.

I felt it almost unfair, with my background, to take part. A smug attitude which burst like a balloon in a thorn bush when someone else scored more marks, a lady who turned out to be a violin teacher. She received from Cedric a small prize — and a celebration kiss.

He didn't appear in the evening's Show, instead filling in at the keyboard in the Buona Notte Bar because someone was still unwell. I sat there a short while with Aunt Dee and Hayden over modest glasses of wine. Hayden knocked his glass over. We didn't say much or stay long. Altogether, it wasn't a hugely satisfactory day.

But in the morning Dubrovnik awaited us, the colourful Croatian port sheltered by its old fortress walls: the snag being that the ship needed to anchor some way out, and bright orange tenders would ferry sightseers ashore. Not a good option for Aunt Ruby, but she wasn't to be put off.

'It's the last one. I'll never see anything like this again at my time of life. I'm coming!'

And she came, being half lifted into the small crowded craft by grinning crew members, with her straw hat askew and her walking-stick a danger to everyone. We set off at quite a speed across the sunlit water, rainbow spray flying as we bumped along. On one side loomed the bulk of the ship that had been home, it seemed, for a long time: on the other, the clustering red roofs and guardian walls of the old City baked in unbroken sunshine. Indeed, even on the water there was scarcely a breath of cooling breeze.

The major tour involved tramping around the City walls, but of course, we hadn't chosen that. Our less arduous trip took us first by coach to a panoramic viewpoint on a lofty hill, where our guide (alas, not 'Emily', but a serious-faced man with rambling and somewhat fractured English) told us historic details about the old Republic of Ragusa. I gave Alicia a couple of nudges, afraid she would fall asleep on her feet.

Back again at the centre-point of the Pile Gate, there followed an on-foot tour to see churches and buildings, and the Cloisters of the Franciscan Monastery with stone arches and green gardens. How Aunt Ruby stood the course I couldn't imagine. She even poked the guide with her stick a couple of times to ask questions.

There was free time to explore the length of the broad main street, bordered on either side by shops and cafés. It was very hot, and everywhere was thronged with tourists. Almost at once Hayden pointed out a café up a steep side-road.

'It's in the shade. Aunt Ruby, you'd like some tea?'

'I really would, my dear.' Her plump face was red and damp, and she hung on to him up the narrow hill between the buildings. But it was indeed out of the sun, and the pavement tables were invitingly spread with blue and white cloths.

Hayden muttered to me, 'I'll stay with her, if you could trot the kids around?'

'Of course. We'll come back to you here. Just keep Aunt Ruby happy!'

I hadn't missed the way he passed

across the menu without even looking at it, nor the painful frown he had worn all morning. Aunt Dee gave me one of her knowing glances which expressed exactly my own thoughts: how much had he actually seen of Dubrovnik? — and between him and Aunt Ruby, who was really helping whom?

The shops were interesting, not cheap, and all of them crowded. We bought souvenir pens, key-rings, photo-calendars: also, in answer to Alicia's pleading, lemon ices all round. Jamie chose, of all things, a Croatian/English dictionary — which gave rise to another of Aunt Dee's comments, this time whispered in my ear.

'Bless his heart, exactly how old is the little chap?'

'Five next month,' I whispered back, 'but he's Hayden's flesh and blood — so they'll enjoy learning Croatian together while other kids and dads play football!'

She nodded and pulled an expressive face. The next moment she added soberly,

'That's always supposing Hayden can read what the book says. You know, he worries me.'

I agreed truthfully, 'Me too.'

At the café once more, we found him sitting with Aunt Ruby quite amicably over emptied teacups and remnants of cake. I ordered cold drinks, and they had just arrived when my phone jangled to announce one of its untimely messages.

'Sorry it's all nearly over for you, hope you've had a really good time . . . '

'Who's that?' demanded Aunt Ruby, from whom you could hide little. 'If it's Tina, ask her if it's rained. I'm sure that Mrs. Kirby opposite won't have watered my pots.'

'It's not Tina. Just a few words from Grant.'

She said 'Ah!' — whatever that meant. There and then I tapped out a rapid reply:

'Thanks, Grant, it's been wonderful! And congratulations to you and Elaine, I'm very happy for you both . . . '

Was it really a blatant lie? I showed Aunt Dee my return message under the table. Being her sensitive and caring self, she would know my thoughts. She would live with me my past sorrows and my new hopes. She would know too that 'moving on' was still so very hard to do.

*　*　*

'I'll never make my case shut,' Alicia said gloomily.

I was having much the same trouble with my own, cramming in bags and bundles bought day by day. As for the giant carriers with Aunt Dee's present, no luggage on earth would contain them.

On this final evening it seemed that the 'Bella Italia', a few days ago so confusing and strange, was all at once pleasantly familiar. So were the faces of acquaintances in neighbouring cabins. The sunny deck and blue pool were enticing. And who would be the next people to sit out on our balcony and watch the shining oceans glide past?

We had a last look at the Photo-shop, and rashly I bought a whole handful of pictures that I had previously declined because my hair looked like a haystack, or Alicia had her tongue out at Jamie, or Aunt Ruby looked too grim. When we prepared for our final dinner, surprisingly, Alicia made a real effort, piling her hair up attractively with the fancy grips Cedric gave her, borrowing a floaty skirt I hadn't got round to wearing.

Her face and arms were golden-brown from our days in the sun. She looked nice. It occurred to me, very late in the day, she looked probably the image of her dead mother?

By our standards, the meal was uneventful. Major Battersby paused by our table to chat in his staccato manner. Kelly-Ann and Joey waved across to us. Jamie practised his vocabulary on Eugenio who had looked after us so patiently.

Indeed, there would be so many memories to carry home along with those bulging suitcases! And tonight would add to them — for in the Grand Farewell Show in the big theatre, Cedric had a special spot of his own. Alone on the stage, with a background of twinkling stars, the light gilding his hair, his face was turned from me but I knew its every feature, every expression.

What music he played I scarcely knew. There was applause, more music, more applause. At the end he came to the front of the stage to take his last bow, a slender figure in a pale-cream jacket with a dark red flower on the lapel.

He saw me then, our eyes meeting as though drawn by some magnetic force. He was beckoning to me, and I stumbled a few steps towards him down the centre aisle. It was all unreal. He tossed his flower down to me.

There was laughter and applause all around, from people who thought the star pianist had just picked out at random a young lady to receive that romantic gesture. They didn't know the truth, as I did. Through the rest of the show I cradled the blood-red carnation in my lap.

I heard Aunt Dee murmur something to her sister, and Aunt Ruby's hissed reply: 'Yes, well, it's the way these Continentals go on! You know, it makes me think of years ago when I was with — '

'I know, my dear, I know,' Aunt Dee hushed her quickly.

The Show moved on to its finale and a line-up of its entertainers. When the tinselled curtains closed for the last time, and the audience began filing and chattering to the exits, I was glad of Aunt Ruby's slowness in moving. We were just at the door, the last to leave, when Cedric came to us.

'Hi! You were great! Best of the lot!' Alicia greeted him.

Aunt Dee agreed, 'We all really enjoyed it. So are you off duty now, Cedric?'

'I'm afraid I'm not. Pierre is still sick, I have to be in the Buona Notte Bar again till late.' He looked at me as he said it, very close to me. 'Lauren, I'm sorry, I hoped we could talk tonight — but I'll see you in the morning, I promise. There's something very special I want to say to you . . . to ask you . . . '

The last words were a murmur, just for me. I nodded. I held on to my red flower.

Somehow the luggage was fastened up and parked outside the cabins for collection, with depressing 'return home' labels attached. Aunt Dee and Hayden seemed to have made their two cabins a joint operation and managed the job between them. For this final occasion we all assembled for a drink and a light snack before bed, looking out at the dark sea under a summer night sky. Jamie was almost asleep on his feet, but perked up enough to wish me a parting, 'Buona sera, a piu tardi!'

'See you later too, Jamie!' I said. It was nice that he looked less of a forlorn waif than when we started out. Despite a few frights along the way, the sea air and sunshine and kindly company must have been beneficial.

In the cabin, Alicia eyed the red flower with envy and asked, 'Are you going to sleep with it under your pillow?'

I said mundanely, 'No, it might squash and spoil the bed.'

As I placed it instead in a tumbler of water she had a further thought: 'Of course, he might have aimed it at me and misfired it! — mightn't he?'

It rained quite a lot that night. I heard raindrops pelting on the balcony, and for the first time the ship seemed to lurch and judder just a little. I dreaded to imagine how Aunt Ruby was faring.

It was still grey and damp when we crammed last minute things into the hand baggage. Despite all her grumbles during these past days, Alicia looked as mournful as the drab sky.

We were due in Venice about ten. Meantime, there was breakfast, the last scramble at the tea and coffee dispensers. Hayden no longer volunteered, so Aunt Dee shared that fraught task with me. Indeed, I wasn't interested in food or drink, just waiting, waiting . . . watching the busy scene around, speaking to people we had come to know, exchanging addresses with Kelly-Ann.

'I'm back at my part-time job in a couple of days,' she bewailed. 'I can't believe it's gone by so fast. And my back looks like it'll peel, I shall sue those sun-cream people if it does . . .'

Major Battersby was hovering in the vicinity of Aunt Dee, and she was very busy checking the disembarkation information. Jamie was writing a goodbye note to Giuseppe. We were almost ready to vacate our chairs when I saw a man approaching us between the tables.

'Morning, Cedric!' Aunt Dee greeted him in her pleasant way. 'Nice to see you. I'm really glad of a chance to say how much we've enjoyed your music, all of us have. The voyage wouldn't have been the same without it!'

'That's very kind of you. I hope all of you have had a happy holiday, it's so sad it must end. But you'll have a little time to see Venice?'

'Oh yes, we shall. And will you have some free time here too, dear? — you deserve it!'

'Yes, I have free time here too today.' He smiled at her, that smile. That smile! . . .

He had a few encouraging words for Alicia, hoping (with one meaning glance at Hayden) that she could continue her music studies — 'and if I had more fans like you, I'd really go places! . . .' As well, he gave her a small photograph inscribed 'To Alicia, Keep practising!'

And then at last, it was my turn. He asked, 'Will you come out on the deck for just a moment? — do you have time?'

I had time. If I were the last passenger left aboard, I would have time.

The sun-loungers so popular through

many basking days were deserted. Just a few people stood at the rails looking at the grey water under that overcast sky. There was still a drizzle of rain in the air. For me, standing beside him, all was still sunshine.

'I wanted to see you alone. I have special things to tell you,' he was saying, his quiet, accented voice never more appealing.

I whispered, 'Yes?' and waited. He wasn't hurrying.

'I do many of these travellings to many places, but — this one has been different. This time I have met you. I think there are many things we share together . . . oh, I'm saying this badly! . . . '

It seemed to me he was saying it very well. I waited again while he sorted out more words. He had hold of my hand, and he bent his head over it to touch it to his lips.

'I want to ask you — I think you may say 'no', but I ask you please to consider hard . . . Lauren, this is a very precious hand, a gifted hand! I ask you, please don't let it waste. When you are home, when all is quiet — *go back to your music*, yes? . . . '

'Oh,' I muttered. 'Music.'

'I'll always remember you, and our times together. I'll look always to see your name at the concert halls. I'm so very happy to have known you . . . '

'I'm happy to have known you too,' my own voice said from worlds away.

The grey of the morning had deepened all at once into a great darkness.

6

'Well, I must say, this is a nice rigmarole,' Aunt Ruby grumbled.

Disembarkation was proceeding. Obviously, a couple of thousand people couldn't leave the cruise liner en masse. We waited at a table with drinks and biscuits, listening for our group number and instructions to be called in the usual succession of languages.

Stunned, empty, tearless, I sat there trying to look interested, trying to hear what people said to me. Half an hour ago, finally vacating the cabin, Alicia had pointed out, 'Your red flower is still in the glass of water.'

'I know. You take it, if you like.'

'Can I really? I've got the photo — '

'Have the flower too.'

'Well, all right.' She dried it carefully on a towel. 'If I press it, it'll keep for ages. If you're sure?'

I had never been more sure of anything.

'How long did you say we've got to wait about for the plane?' Aunt Ruby was going on. Her exertions of yesterday seemed to have caught up with her. 'It's raining, Dee. My rheumatics are playing up.'

'The flight isn't till this evening. But this is Venice, dear.'

'I don't care where it is, it's still raining!'

We were indeed a cheery party, quite apart from my own state of mind. Jamie, after giving his farewell note to Guiseppi (a strange little friendship) looked on the verge of tears. Hayden had just received another lecture about sunburn from Aunt Ruby — and countered it with a somewhat curt, 'Well, I won't burn any more this morning, Mrs. Pym.' He sat next to me with a silent and immovable frown.

In fact, I fully shared Aunt Ruby's feelings about these hours of waiting limbo. I wanted now just to get on that plane, to be far away from these last dreamlike days! The real world was out there somewhere. Perhaps it was my only salvation. Back in London there must be no more drifting, seeing Tina off to work each morning from the flat — with my main goal of a new day to search the shops for a DVD or book that might amuse Grant . . . to be early at the hospital for visiting time . . . to be polite to Elaine . . .

We did get around to disembarking, at last. Safely ashore, we were able to park our assorted clutter of luggage (including those rather accursed cushions) in trolleys in a secure location, to be collected later when we boarded a coach shuttle to the airport. And meanwhile, Aunt Dee insisted, we must all go by water-bus to St. Mark's Square, because it must on no account be missed, even in the rain.

'And the rain's stopping! We've several hours for Venice — and there's some blue sky breaking through.' She pointed cheerfully upwards, despite the rest of us looking rather as though we wished Venice would go and jump into one of its own canals.

Privately she had murmured to me, 'Did you and Cedric have any plans of your own, dear? Because that's fine, we can all meet up later.'

I answered her briefly, 'No plans. Not ever.'

For a moment her kind hand was on my arm. 'I did wonder. I'm so very sorry.'

'Don't be. I just — made a mistake. He was trying to help with my music problems and I misunderstood — I suppose I was upset about Grant and I thought — '

She said gently, 'Don't blame yourself. He's a very attractive young man, and he obviously thought you were special. It was plain to see.'

'But he didn't want to get involved. Well, fair enough!'

'It happens,' she whispered.

She might have added that I had been caught on the rebound from

Grant, or that I had let myself dream too many dreams about a handsome face and some beautiful music. I was glad she said no more. I couldn't trust my voice to answer.

The water-bus bore us briskly away, past several massive cruise liners, our late home just about the largest. I couldn't tell which of those innumerable balconies had been mine. Really, I didn't want to know.

'Cheer up,' Aunt Dee was rallying Alicia, 'there'll be some nice shops and cafés. Let's make the most of it, eh?'

Alicia shrugged a laconic, 'Whatever.'

It hadn't been easy to get Aunt Ruby on to the water-bus, and it wasn't easy to get her off again. Whether it was reaction to all her recent experiences, regret at going home, or simply those rampant 'rheumatics', she was in one of her most fractious moods. If we wanted to go gallivanting around Italy today, she said, we should have parked her with the luggage at the shipping terminal till we returned.

Back on dry land, Aunt Dee was soon announcing unnecessarily, 'The Piazza San Marco! What do you think?'

With its surround of picturesque architecture, the Cathedral, the vast paved space where birds swooped and clustered, even despite the damp and the tourists it was magnificent. I said so, as no-one else seemed inclined to answer. Groups of café tables were blossoming as the weather brightened, and stalls were selling food for the pigeons. Dawdling sightseers were taking photographs of the surroundings and each other.

Aunt Ruby began wearily, 'All very nice, Dee, but I'll have to sit down somewhere if you want to walk about . . .'

'Just turn around, dear,' her sister interrupted with sudden gleeful excitement. 'Turn around! Hold on to me and take a deep breath!'

I saw a man approaching us, an elderly man, not very tall, lined of face and snow-white of hair, somewhat rotund of figure. Aunt Ruby saw him too. She was suddenly as pale as a ghost.

'No, you're not dreaming, Ruby,' Aunt Dee said gently.

He was near to us now, and he smiled at the shocked old lady, holding out a hand to her.

'How are you, cara mia? . . . you know me? . . . '

Aunt Ruby breathed, 'Mario?'

'Si! And I would know you any-where!'

In my present emotional state, I felt tears tugging at my eyes. I struggled hard with them as I watched and listened. It seemed Aunt Dee had arranged this amazing reunion, the 'special reason' she had mentioned to me for taking her sister along on our travels. If for a moment there was disappointment in my mind that my imagined picture of the artist — a tall, darkly handsome Romeo of a man — had been displaced by today's real life, somewhat 'lived-in' Mario Amato, I soon pushed it aside.

He was saying that Aunt Dee had told him all about Ruby's long marriage to Tom, that he was so sorry she had lost the husband who made her happy for many years. Aunt Ruby said shakily that Tom was the best, the very best. 'And — and you, Mario? — '

'I've been ill. For years ill, not good. Now I am better — and more better to see you again!'

He kissed her gently, and offered her a flower. It was a deep red rose.

A red flower. The tears finally spilled over in my eyes. The whole scene became as hazy to me as it ever could be to Hayden, standing in embarrassed silence beside me.

There followed introductions all round, hand shakes and hugs, and then we were being led to a café table already reserved for us. Across the Square, Aunt Ruby held on to Mario's arm, and the rest of us followed in a jumbled crocodile. Aunt Dee was almost prancing, explaining to Alicia exactly who the stranger was: 'Mario

Amato was quite a famous artist in his day, Ally, and years ago — nearly sixty years! — he was poor dear Ruby's sweetheart. She modelled for him, if you can believe that! Well, I discovered he was living in Venice, I fixed up this for her as a big surprise!'

Alicia said, 'Cool.' It was at that exact moment that the sun broke through.

Trailing in the rear, I dabbed at those insistent tears. The warmth of the sunshine didn't reach me.

★ ★ ★

The café table was round, spread with a cream cloth, and centred with a bowl of more red roses. By the time I was seated there between Hayden and Alicia, I had made a huge effort to pull myself together.

Aunt Ruby was elderly and ailing, and today would bring a brief sunburst into her life, a memory to cherish through cold wintertimes and declining years. It would bring joy as well to her sister, to have brought it about. So, indeed, it had to be a celebration! I found myself chatting, asking questions, laughing, as the wine and fruit juices and cappuccino circulated, along with platters of delectable pastries. I mopped up discreetly for Hayden when he upset his coffee.

But it wasn't too long before Aunt Dee was yanking Jamie from his seat: 'Come on, it's just one Euro for some food for these hungry pigeons. Let's see if they'll eat out of our hands!'

The boy looked doubtfully at his father, but he let my Aunt lead him away. The parting wink she gave me was a clear enough hint. I also got to my feet.

'And I must get some last minute shopping, an engagement present for some friends. Alicia, please come and help me! And you, Hayden, I need lots of advice.'

Alicia muttered ungraciously, 'Do I have to?' He frowned at me in silence. The Jardines were guaranteed to rain on any parade, but not Aunt Ruby's if I could help it. I told Mario, 'We'll be back soon,' and he nodded and smiled.

It was a nice smile, with something special about it. I didn't want to think about special smiles at present. Really, I didn't want to think about anything at all.

'This is really lovely for Aunt Ruby, isn't it?' I said with somewhat artificial brightness. 'Worth all her trials and tribulations of the holiday! — even the food!'

Hayden said, 'Indeed.' Which killed that topic stone dead. I didn't attempt another.

We were an uneasy trio setting off across the Square. There was a chill in the air that the strengthening Venetian warmth couldn't shift. Alicia plodded sulkily on one side of me, and on my other side Hayden was squinting painfully in the sun. Without knowing at all where I was going, I led the way around some back turnings lined with fascinating shop windows, displaying clothes and jewellery, attractive bags, arrays of strange and colourful masks.

The idea of buying Grant and Elaine a gift really had been a sudden brainwave excuse to afford Aunt Ruby and Mario some privacy, but it did need doing. In fact, I bought almost the first thing I saw, a jug and tumbler set in beautiful ruby glass with gold rims.

'All done!' I told my indifferent companions. 'Does anyone else need to do any shopping?' I whispered to Alicia, 'I've some currency to use up, if you want to get your Dad something?'

She said gruffly, 'No thanks!'

'Then something for the Aunts?'

'I already did. A little vase. In Istanbul.'

'Oh. That's nice,' I said lamely. There was no way of guessing what she might do. At least I knew better than to suggest we look at any more impressive architecture.

'Well! No point in trailing round if no-one's interested — but we don't want to play gooseberry in that café.

Let's sit down a while. And an ice would be nice, my treat!'

By pure chance there was a convenient back street which ended abruptly at the waterside. It was edged by weathered walls, high casements with bright flowers spilling from their balconies, a notice about gondola rides. No-one was about there just now. We had recently passed a sales kiosk under a striped sunshade, and I backpedalled to spend the leftover coins.

On a stone bench by a wall we sat in a tense row: it seemed to me more and more that the atmosphere was building up ominously to some sort of human thunderstorm. I tried not to splatter my cone of gorgeous Italian icecream, while Alicia sucked noisily at a fruit lolly, her feet sprawled beside kicked-off trainers. Hayden just sat there.

I said at length, 'Phew, it's getting warm. We could move over there in the shade if it's bothering you, Hayden.'

'No. If you've an umbrella handy to shelter my nose. Aunt Ruby thinks I should change my name to Rudolph.'

I giggled nervously. Perhaps I was wrong about an impending storm? 'It's not that vivid! — quite a tasteful terra cotta shade. Just tell her it's the sun-kissed look — '

There, I broke off abruptly. Alicia had just tossed her lolly-wrapper and a couple of sticky tissues carelessly on to the pavement. It stopped Hayden's attempt at good humour in its tracks. He fairly barked at her, 'Alicia, pick that up! — *Now*!'

'It's only paper. It'll blow away.'

'It's litter. Only ignorant layabouts leave litter around. Pick it up!'

She gave a deep sigh and began an exasperatingly slow process of putting her shoes back on. So trivial an incident, so very trivial — but an eddy of breeze caught the unsightly objects and twirled them along, and Hayden's patience seemed to snap. As he started forward to gather them up, I saw him move from glaring sun to deep shadow, and his sudden reaction to whatever dizzily blurred picture he was seeing.

The rubbish drifted again. It evaded his reaching hand.

There were stone steps dropping steeply to the water. Beneath them, it looked deep and sullen and unforgiving. Another stumbling step or two and he would surely fall head first — to crack his skull on the rough stone, and slip straight down into the murky depths.

My lightning instinct was to scream a warning, to rush forward. But I didn't do either. There was another instinct that made me stifle the cry, somehow force myself to sit there zombie-like, silent and still. My heart raced in horror at the gamble I was taking. I scarcely even dared to watch.

For might Alicia just go on sitting here too? Would she even care what happened to this man she professed to hate so bitterly? If she really were the cold-blooded young schemer he believed, wouldn't she even chalk this up as an unexpected and rather amusing bonus? . . .

'Stop! — stay there!' a voice shrilled. It wasn't my voice. 'Stay there! — Daddy, *don't move!* — '

It was a split-second warning she shouted. It was a split-second dive she made to fling her arms round him even as he seemed to be losing his balance. The man and the child ended up in a tangled heap on the steps, only just above the water.

I was shaking so much, after that huge risk I had taken, that for a moment I still went on sitting like a frozen statue. Only dimly I was aware of Alicia sobbing and sobbing — and between the sobs were broken words, 'I'm sorry . . . I'm sorry . . . ' over and over again.

* * *

A young man and a girl were running up to us, their rapid Italian obviously asking if they could help. Then some other people materialised, trying to assist. I signified that we were 'okay', a helpfully universal term, adding a few 'grazies' and 'grazie milles'. I thought absurdly, we needed Jamie here to help us out.

Somehow we were back on the stone seat, all of us utterly shaken. Alicia was still sobbing fitfully, her face blotched with tears. I saw — if I could believe what I saw — that Hayden had a consoling arm around her.

I said awkwardly, 'Er — hem! — perhaps I'll wander off for a while?'

'Don't go!' Alicia clutched at me. 'Please stay here! But — were you really just going to sit there and let him fall down those steps? He might have bashed his brains in!'

'Yes, I know. Ally, I'm really sorry, I just — froze. Here!' I passed her a bundle of tissues. 'Just cry it out. Cry everything out.'

The tallest of tall orders, perhaps. And yet it almost seemed that might happen. She couldn't stop crying, the tears of a lonely, grieving, resentful, misunderstood child. And words were coming too, still broken by those racking sobs. The words weren't for me but for the man beside her, leaning his head back against the wall. The shock and pain in his thin, fair face made it haggard and drawn.

I felt like an intruder as she remembered the day her mother died, the Nancy Jardine I had heard of a few times. There was a disastrous quarrel in the house that day between Hayden and his wife, the biggest of several. With her ear to their door, Alicia had listened and trembled. As so often, the trouble was about herself. This stern stranger who had come into her life and so changed it, kept insisting in his chilly way, 'That child must learn to behave, it's no good being soft with her, always giving in to her the way you do!'

And her beloved mother, in deepest distress and anger, flung out of the house and into the little silver car Hayden had just bought for her, and drove off down the road. Alicia remembered the small shiny vehicle disappearing round the corner. It never returned. Within half an hour it was a mangled wreck. The woman driving it died at its brand new wheel.

Dear heaven above, so like Grant and myself, so very like! So we had stormed and raged before he drove away. Grant had lived — but part of him had died. And part of me had died with him.

So well I could understand how all Alicia's pent-up grief for her mother was mixed with anger against Hayden, and with a huge burden of personal shame and guilt. It was a crushing weight upon her young shoulders.

She accused him now quite fiercely through her tears, 'You always moaned at me! — if I ever tried to please you — oh no, oh no, you just always moaned! — '

'Alicia,' Hayden said quietly, 'you have your mother's quick temper — and her eyes, and her face . . . quite often I've found it hard to have you near me . . . '

'That's not my fault! I didn't choose

182

the way I look, did I?'

'No, you didn't. I'm sorry. I'm very sorry.'

She swept on as though she hadn't heard, 'And then there was that absolutely foul exam. Why do you think I wanted so much to go in for it?'

'I had my suspicions. I've told you about them.'

'Yes, a mean trick to get you thrown out of the school. And that's not true! I was just so tired of how things were at home, like — like living inside a freezer! — I just wanted you to be pleased for once. I thought you'd be pleased if I did well at those horrible maths. And I did do well! And then — you said I'd cheated.'

'Didn't you?'

'No, I didn't! I've tried to tell you, but would you listen? — would *anyone* listen? — '

She was breaking down into incoherence. I said gently, 'Ally, darling, we're listening. Just calm down and tell us.'

'Well, there's this girl — Olivia Parke,

she's a lot older than me — '

Hayden intervened, 'Yes, a very gifted student. She has a place at Cambridge.'

'Yes, well, she was nice to me, we often got the same bus home — and I used to go in her house lots of times to talk to her Mum. Sometimes I went there by myself if Olivia had to be late at school, I made tea for her and took in cherry-almond squares from the bakers, she used to eat three straight off! . . . She's blind, did you know that? I mean, really blind . . . '

'I didn't know that.' Hayden sounded utterly shocked.

'Olivia's a wizard at maths, I told her how much I wanted to pass the exam, and she coached me. Hours and hours, after school. You were doing extra classes, Jamie was at Mrs. Harper's till you picked him up . . . I worked and worked, Olivia set me questions and I used to do them in bed and then she marked them . . . ' She took a deep tremulous breath. 'I thought you'd be really thrilled if I did well, you — you might even like me a bit more . . . '

There was a long moment of silence as the words trailed away. When she spoke again it was a very small, sad voice in the quiet.

'But you said I cheated. You locked up my Mum's piano. It — it's still locked — '

Even more I felt an intruder, most of all as I stole a glance at Hayden — and saw plainly the tears on his face. Though those pale ice-blue eyes didn't see clearly, they could still weep.

But if I must be part of this agonising laying bare of souls, perhaps I could help just a little. I said softly, 'Ally, I know your Dad isn't always — he's just not very easy to talk to — and you fought back by behaving badly to annoy him, I understand that. But tell us, why didn't Olivia speak up for you over the exam? She knew your paper was genuine!'

'Oh, she'd left the school, you see. She and her Mum went to stay with her Gran in Canada for the summer, her Gran was ill. She sent me a card, and she rang me to ask about the exam. I just said I did all right. Her Gran had just died, she was awfully upset, I — I couldn't tell her what really happened — '

'Of course you couldn't,' I whispered.

She was calmer now, mopping her eyes, pushing back damp tangles of long dark hair. It was Hayden who found the next words. His head was bowed down on his hands, his face hidden. His voice was very near to breaking.

'Alicia, I don't know what to say to you. I just hope you can forgive me for hurting you so much. I hope — perhaps — we can try to start over again? . . . if you'd like to do that? . . . '

'Well, I've been pretty gross to you too,' she insisted quite matter of factly. 'And I thought Auntie Megan was just fussing like she always does — but you couldn't really see those steps just now, could you? I ought to have known.'

'I did see them. Not well enough to

avoid falling down them if you hadn't saved me.'

'But — ' She turned suddenly to burrow into him. 'Can't the hospital make you better? You're not going to be like Mrs. Parke is, are you?'

'Probably not. It's not certain — but probably not.' He was holding her close to him now, rocking her gently like a baby. 'Don't worry about it too much. Whatever happens, we'll manage. So cheer up, Ally. At least I know I'll have someone to give me tea and cherry-almond squares? . . . '

Locked in their long delayed embrace, half smiling, half crying, their tears had started again. They were more gentle and relieving tears that fell now, his and hers.

And mine were falling too. Mine too.

* * *

We walked back to the Square very slowly. It seemed as though a whole day had passed since we left the café table,

187

but really it wasn't so very long. Long enough to shake the world on its axis for two troubled people — though I didn't delude myself that all their battles were over. It would take more time for the anger and pain to filter away.

I was thrilled to have played some small part in this reconciliation, as my dear Aunt Dee had originally asked me. I was thrilled too for Aunt Ruby, who had been so kind to me during this holiday. There wasn't too much else to be thrilled about today.

On our way back Alicia was very quiet, plainly drained by the emotional scene. But I noticed she was holding fast to Hayden's hand. I plodded along just behind them with my package of Venetian glassware for Grant and Elaine. Grant and Elaine! — there was nothing I could do about that. And tonight I would be back in London and Cedric Raphael would still be here in Italy, soon to sail off again into the blue with his music and his special smile.

No, it was time to abandon maudlin self-pity! Tomorrow I would start hawking my Mediterranean tan around the employment agencies to find a job, any sort of job! And religiously I would visit the Aunts every weekend so Hayden Jardine couldn't accuse me again of neglect as he did at our first meeting . . .

'So there you are!' Aunt Dee beamed at us. She was just returning with Jamie towards the restaurant, both of them carrying shopping, and Jamie ran eagerly to his father. 'Had a nice time, my dears? Lauren, you look — '

She peered at me, seeming unable to describe how I looked.

'I bought a nice present for Grant. Really nice — if I can get it home in one piece.'

'Good!' She edged closer as we followed the Jardine trio. 'Tell me, am I losing my marbles at last, or was Ally holding his hand just now?'

'She was! Look, she is again. I know it's hard to believe, it's a long story

— but we've had a big crisis. I'll explain it all later.'

She said softly, 'Thank you. It means quite a lot to me.'

The Square was busier now, more people strolling in the sunshine, more pigeons, more chairs filled at the cafes, a trio of musicians wafting their pleasant melodies abroad. At our round table with the dominating red roses, we found Aunt Ruby and Mario sitting together over emptied coffee cups. He had been showing her some old photographs, still spread around. She gave us a very benign welcome back.

But we weren't to remain there long. Aunt Dee rallied us all briskly, 'Now then, folks, we've only a few hours here, so no wasting time. Gondola rides, that's a must!'

'That's a nice thought, Dee,' Aunt Ruby demurred, 'but I'm really not sure I can — '

'Of course you can. Can't she, Mario?'

'Si! I go with you, Ruby. Is a

beautiful experience. Meraviglioso!'

That seemed to change her mind. I heard Jamie echo thoughtfully, 'Meraviglioso?'

Of course, Mario knew where to go to hire those most picturesque and romantic craft. We trailed along in a straggling bunch.

'This is how we'll do it, everyone,' Aunt Dee was saying. When she was in organizing mode, things happened. Of course, her sister and Mario must be together — and after something of a struggle to get Aunt Ruby aboard, she was sitting there like a queen in the high-prowed, decorated boat, propped on cushions with the artist's steadying arm around her. The sun shone on them as the gondola swayed gently away.

'Bless her grumpy old heart,' Aunt Dee murmured. 'Wasn't it worth all we've been through — even the garlic — to see the look on her face?'

I suggested, 'You don't think she'll be canal-sick in a gondola?'

'Not even Ruby. Definitely not today!'

It was nice that we had just met up at the waterside with Kelly-Ann's family, who were trying to calm Joey down and decide whether to chance a ride. Aunt Dee settled the matter for them immediately.

'Of course you must! — you can't miss this, can you, Joey? . . . Come on, Kelly-Ann, we'll go shares. Three children (excuse me, Alicia!) and three adults.'

Joey had pounced with glee on Jamie. Kelly-Ann's sober-faced husband Rob was busy with his assortment of cameras. But I saw Alicia hesitate for a long moment and then give Hayden a nudge.

'Do you mind? Will you be all right? I don't mind staying with you.'

'Of course I'll be all right. Please go. Enjoy it.'

She still lingered doubtfully, but Aunt Dee hustled her along.

Which left one vacant waiting boat, with its lithe-figured, white-shirted proprietor looking expectantly at Hayden and me standing there together.

'Shall we just sit down on that bench over there?' I suggested rather wearily. 'Unless it really appeals to you?'

He said in his chilly way, 'I believe Aunt Dee has already reserved the boat for us.'

I muttered, 'Oh well. Whatever.' (I had, of course, cabin-shared with Alicia for several days.)

The gondolier gave me a charming smile to match his graceful craft, and a supporting hand aboard. Hayden needed the hand more than I did. We sat primly side by side, as the push of the long pole steered us smoothly and silently out on to the water.

And indeed, after a very little while I was glad I agreed to come. The gliding boat, the colours of the waterside buildings reflected in mirror-images of salmon-pink and brown and white, the bridges and flower-decked balconies, the shadows where the water turned to mysterious darkness lapping weathered old walls — all of it was like a dream, a hauntingly beautiful painting come to life.

The spell of Venice wasn't to be denied. Even to my sad and silent observing, it wasn't.

I was aware all at once of a tentative hand touching my arm. Hayden was breaking a long silence to say, 'Lauren, I want to thank you for all your help to Alicia. And for your — shall we say, mediation services — between the two of us . . . ' ('Mediation services'? — did he have to make me sound like an official social worker?) 'I'm afraid it can't have been easy.'

'It wasn't. If you really want to know, I've often felt like knocking your heads together!'

He said quietly, 'I'm not surprised.'

'But there again, I've found out how very easy it is to get a wrong idea in your mind and let it grow and grow. I'm afraid it's happened to me twice over in quick succession! — '

I didn't mean to be saying any of this, but somehow the words kept coming.

And somehow it was a relief to give them voice.

'I had the wrong idea about starting a music partnership with Grant. I was trying to turn the clock back — you can't ever do that, can you? And I had the wrong idea about Cedric Raphael. He just wanted to be a good friend, but I read a lot more into it. I suppose because I was — feeling sorry for myself . . . ' I paused a moment to steady my voice. 'It wasn't his fault, I'm sure he didn't mean to hurt me. He was just — trying to get me back to the piano again — '

'I think he was absolutely right.'

'Oh! You do?' I exclaimed in surprise at the quiet, decisive words.

'Certainly. It wasn't just a career you worked hard to achieve, was it? You loved what you were doing, it was your whole life. But if you can't face the idea of performing at present, because of personal tragedies — couldn't you start by teaching?'

'I don't know. I've never thought

seriously about that.'

'Then think. Think hard! 'The Lauren Roache Piano Masterclass'? — mightn't it be an answer? I've always found teaching very rewarding.'

'Teaching,' I still mused aloud. 'Well, yes, I suppose I could do that?'

I looked into his face close beside me, serious as ever: the high forehead, the well-formed mouth that seldom smiled, the pale fair-lashed eyes that were puckered up to look back into mine — but after all, maybe they were more clear and kind than just glacially cold?

'I could do that!' I repeated quite excitedly. 'I'll investigate as soon as I'm home, I promise! And — now we're into confessions, I must tell you another foolish idea I had. Aunt Ruby lost some jewellery, I was almost sure Alicia had taken it. She had a good opportunity. But this morning it turned up when all the drawers were cleared out, Aunt Dee said it was caught up somehow at the back. I feel awful about that.'

He nodded soberly. 'I'm afraid I'd have thought much the same. Yesterday, I would.'

Yesterday was a world away, for both of us. I sat still and quiet, until I murmured, 'Oh, just look at this beautiful bridge, isn't that a picture? . . . '

He obviously wasn't listening or looking, his mind still on all we had just been saying.

'Don't ever reproach yourself. Not ever. You and your Aunt Dee are two very special people.'

'Oh!' I felt sudden colour rise in my face. 'Of course, Aunt Dee is! — but — '

'You too,' he said deliberately. 'You too. I'd have said this to you before, only I thought you were — spoken for. Twice over.'

'Oh!' I mumbled foolishly again. He still sounded rather as though he was telling Form Four to pay attention or stay in after school. Maybe that didn't matter too much?

'I've tried very hard to keep my distance these past few days,' he was going on. 'You remember that Old Tyme evening?'

'Of course, the night we had — er, a slight disagreement?'

'No, the night I held you in my arms . . . and realised how much I was coming to care for you. Lauren, I know we've had our disagreements, but I believe that's because we haven't understood each other very well. That's in the past. As for the future — I haven't a great deal to offer, a big struggle to get my career back to where it was — quite apart from these wretched health problems, and of course two extra-demanding children. But — if you'll permit, when we get home, I'd like to keep seeing you. Often. Very often? . . . '

'I'm sure the children will be fine! — both of them! — ' I was stammering now in utter confusion. 'And you're a strong person, Denny, you'll get through all your problems somehow. But I'm afraid I'd just provide you with extra ones! I'm nursing two broken hearts — if that's possible! — and there's the music thing, it — it won't be easy, so . . . '

'So you grieve for your lost hopes and dreams, I know,' he said gently. 'I still grieve for Nancy. I'll always grieve for her. I'll always grieve for my troubles with Alicia, always blame myself. We're two hurt people who've made mistakes. Perhaps we could heal one another, if you'd like to try? . . . Would you mind if I kiss you?'

I wondered whether this was real or only part of our fairytale surroundings. I was wondering too how I had ever thought those eyes were only steely-cold, when there could be this tenderness and sincerity in them, and something almost like adoration. I mumbled, 'Yes, I — I suppose you can. If you really want to?'

He said, 'I want to.'

Perhaps, during these past days, my vision had been even dimmer than his. I hadn't realised what should have been so clear: the times when the true humanity and compassion of his nature shone through in his patient kindness and concern with Aunt Ruby — the unstinting care he gave Jamie, the tears he had shed an hour ago for Alicia's wrongs — and the times when he had seemed strangely close to me, when that barrier of his stern, remote self-sufficiency had crumbled away. Always I had been too distracted by other events to perceive what was there for the seeing.

His first kiss was just a touch on my forehead. The second, lingering, caressing, was on my lips. Held close to him, I was just conscious of some indescribable mingling of excitement and tranquillity. The nearness of him, the colours and the flowers around us, the movement of the gliding boat, were merged together in a dreamlike haze.

I was just aware of some sort of sigh of satisfaction from the gondolier who was so deftly propelling us along this magical stream. I saw too, a little way ahead, another gondola with Aunt Dee